SEVERED THINGS

STEPHEN ROSS

BLACK PARROT BOOKS
San Diego, California

To request permissions, contact the publisher at blackparrotbooks@gmail.com.

The Black Parrot Books name and logo are trademarks of Black Parrot Books.

This is a work of fiction. The names, characters, places, and incidents are fictitious and the product of the author's imagination. Any resemblance to actual people, living or dead, or to businesses, companies, events, institutions, or locales is completely coincidental.

Book Cover & Design © 2021 by Stephen Ross
Cover Design by Donika Mishineva
www.artofdonika.com

2021 Black Parrot Books Paperback Edition.

ISBN 978-0-9970876-8-0 (eBook)
ISBN 978-0-9970876-7-3 (paperback)
Library of Congress Control Number: 2021909854

*Thanks to Philip Marlowe, Sam Spade, and
Lew Archer.*

E & A always.

Chapter 1

I SAT IN the only chair in the place, an overstuffed piece of garbage a bum wouldn't sit on, drinking my coffee and looking out the only window in an otherwise soulless room. It was a clear day, and the sky to the east bled dusty orange to light yellow to gray and finally blue. It looked nice. I needed that because you don't see much nice in my line of work. Just then, the phone rang, slapping me out of the only peace I'd had in forty-eight hours. God, I've got to get a new line of work, but at fifty-six, good luck with that.

I answered the phone, "This is Nolan."

"Boss, it's me, Petuski."

"I know that. And stop calling me boss. You're, unfortunately, supposed to be my partner."

"Yeah, I know. It just comes out natural 'cause your so much older than me."

"Thanks for that."

"You're welcome."

"Shut up. Why'd ya call?"

"Well, grab your dick. We got another one."

"Shit."

"I come in early, and the captain pulled me into his office and give me the lowdown."

"It's came and gave."

"What?"

"Nothing."

"Can you swing by the station and get me? The captain wants us on it pronto."

"Yeah, sure. Where are we going?"

"It's by a dirt road off Route Fourteen. Just down from the Hobson place."

I hung up and stood by the window downing the last of my coffee. The sky was mostly yellow and blue now, but some clouds were doing their best to make animal shapes to the northeast. I figured it was an omen.

I stuck my arms through a clean shirt, not pressed, but clean, and threw on the same suit I'd been playing detective in the past two days. It was my best one. Sure, the sleeves were a bit frayed, one of the buttons hung lower than the other, and there was a noticeable stain on the right shoulder where the drunk I hauled in last week let tobacco drool slip from his lips. But, hey, on a small-town detective's salary, a new suit was the last thing on my mind.

I grabbed my keys, wallet, last pack of Old Golds, and headed out the door, snatching my fedora off the wall rack on the way out. The neighbor's cat, a yellow and gray number that looked like it never won a fight, tried to slip between my legs and make my place home. A swift sweep with my right foot changed its mind in a hurry and sent it airborne for a good four feet. As cats always do, it landed on all fours, unharmed, and hightailed it to the little old lady hanging wash in the backyard. She gave me a scowl but didn't say anything.

There was a chill in the October air, so I raised the collar on my coat. The canterbury

green 1950 Ford Fordor was parked on the
street in front of my building, right where I left
it not more than an hour ago. It looked more
undercover than I did. But that was good. No
one knew we were coming unless the cherry
light was stuck on top.

I lit a cigarette, started the engine, and drove
to the station. Petuski was standing on the curb,
drinking one of his God-awful root beers. I
pulled up next to him, and when he reached for
the door, I hit the gas, causing him to spill some
of his drink. I braked a couple feet away and let
him get in.

"Darn it, boss, why do you pull that stuff?"

"Because I can. Did you bring your shield?"

"Of course."

"Your gun?"

"Aw, come off it. It's too early for your she-
nanigans."

I gave a chuckle and said, "Do you have an
address?"

"No. It's a rural spot just past mile marker
seven."

Petuski finished his soda, leaned over against
the window, and shut his eyes. The ride out was
quiet. I like that. It was still too early for most
folks to be going in to work or heading out to
wherever they go. The only obstacle was a
farmer driving his tractor half on the road and
half off. I made it around him and didn't see another car until a flashing red light appeared on
the side of the road ahead. I turned off the
highway and onto a dirt road, more of a path,
really, and Petuski's head shot up.

"What?"

"Settle down, angel. We're here."

The first person I saw was Lila Racine. That woman had curves I'd never seen before. What she did for a cop uniform was almost obscene. But I liked it. Unfortunately, she was twenty-three, which made me invisible. Probably just as well, given how my marriage turned out. I have no desire to put myself through that again. Ever! Petuski has the hots for her, but what a dame like her would see in that goofball, I can't imagine.

I got out of the car. Petuski ran a comb through his Brylcreemed hair and stepped out, his cheeks tinted with the glow of love.

I walked over to Lila and said, "Well, Lila, what've we got?"

She looked down, cleared her throat, and in a soft voice, said, "Well, sir, we got another one."

I knew what she meant, but I wanted to hear her say it, so I said, "Another one what, Lila?"

She swallowed hard, glanced up at me and back down again, and said even softer this time, "A penis."

I gave her a shocked look and said, "No, Lila. What's gonna happen to the human race if this keeps up?"

"I don't know, sir."

"Well let's not give up on us yet. Where is it?"

She pointed to a clump of grass just off the road where two cops stood silently looking at a bloody object that could have easily been mistaken for a Ball Park frank dipped in ketchup.

I looked at the two cops and said, "What are

you two clowns doing so close to the deceased? You're mucking up my crime scene. Get back out here and watch where you step."

I saw an old man and a cocker spaniel standing on the other side of the road and asked Lila, "Who's the dog lover?"

"That's Mr. Talvers. Bud Talvers. He's the one who found the ... object."

"Lila, why don't you and the boys spread out and see if you can find the body this thing was attached to while I talk to Talvers?"

"Yes, sir."

As I walked toward Talvers, I saw slack-jawed Petuski staring at Lila's backside as she combed through the brush. "Petuski, wake up. Grab the camera and snap some shots of that thing."

Petuski came back to the moment and said, "Will do, boss."

"And stop with the boss."

"Yes, boss."

I rolled my eyes and stepped up to Talvers. The dog growled, I growled back, and extended my hand to the old man.

"Mr. Talvers, I'm Detective Nolan. I understand you're the one who found the member."

"Well, sir, it was actually Sandy who found it."

"Who's Sandy?"

He pointed to the dog and said, "We were out for our early morning constitutional when Sandy went off the path and into the grass. I didn't pay any attention until I saw she had something in her mouth."

"She had it in her mouth?"

"Yes, sir. I immediately told her to drop it, which she did. She's very well trained that way. The missus and I worked real hard with her ever since she was a puppy. From the very first day—"

"OK. I get it. She's a good mutt."

"Dog."

"Whatever. Did you see anyone around here? Anyone on the road? Any cars? Anything that looked suspicious?"

"No, sir. It was just me and Sandy."

I looked at the old man and wondered if he'd had the same English teacher as Petuski. I guessed not since he was at least three times Petuski's age.

Continuing, I said, "Did Sandy move the thing from where she found it?"

"Oh, no, sir. She dropped it right where she found it. I'm sure of that."

I pulled out my notebook, took down Talvers information, and sent him on his way.

Petuski walked up and said he'd taken several pictures from all angles and didn't see anything else worth noting.

I looked over at the thing and said, "How do you explain this?"

Petuski, in all his brilliance, shrugged his shoulders and said, "Maybe the guy was just a dick."

I have to admit I cracked a smile with that one. Petuski tries hard to be funny, and sometimes he is. Mostly irritating, but sometimes funny.

I put on some gloves, pulled an evidence bag

from my pocket, and walked back to the victim. I carefully picked up the weenie, dropped it in the bag, and put it in my pocket. On my way back to the dirt road, I saw a bare patch of ground with a distinctive footprint in it. It was wedge-shaped, with a pointy toe and a small circular puncture in the dirt where the heel would be. Definitely a woman's shoe. I told Petuski to get some shots of it. He did.

Upon further inspection of the area, I found a partial tire print on the side of the road. There wasn't much, maybe six inches long, and half a tire wide. Next to it was a filter-tipped cigarette butt with lipstick on it. I thought that interesting. Could a dame be involved?

Petuski snapped a few more pictures, I put the butt in a bag, and we drove back to the station.

Chapter 2

I DROPPED PETUSKI off at the station to get the pictures developed and took the severed member to Doc Williams. He's one of a handful of MDs in town and serves as the county coroner.

Doctor Charles "Charlie" Williams is older than dirt and the only doc willing to serve as coroner. He's no forensic pathologist but does a fair job with the basics. The other docs are either younger, with families and busy practices, or simply have no interest in the work. Charlie's wife died years ago, and his practice has steadily declined ever since. The twenty-five bucks he gets for each coroner case keeps him supplied with the medication that has kept him going for the past many years—Mogen David MD 20/20 fortified wine. The red grape variety has been both his savior and his downfall. I always found it interesting that although he's not Jewish, he picked a kosher wine as his medication of choice. And the MD appellation makes it especially apropos.

I rang the bell and stepped into the office. Charlie was sitting behind his desk, reading the latest copy of *Argosy Magazine.* He's a pulp fiction nut and reads every issue from cover to cover.

Charlie dropped the read on the desk and said, "Vince Nolan, I figured you'd be coming by."

"Yeah, well, I got more work for ya."

"Really? What's up?"

I laid the bag with the severed evidence on his desk and filled him in on the details we had so far.

"Oh, my, this is not good."

"You're telling me. If the last one didn't do it, this oughta shrivel scrotums around the county."

"Speaking of which, I have the results of my investigation on the one you dropped off yesterday."

"Great. What did you find?"

Charlie opened the drawer of his desk and brought out the black, spiral notebook where he keeps his notes. He flipped through a few pages and then looked up.

"Looks like the penis is from a Caucasian male."

"Really? And here I thought it was from a female."

"Hold on. There's more."

"I hope so."

"The blood on the penis is O positive, which is the most common type. Thirty-seven percent of the population has it. It's the only type I found, so I assume all the blood is from the dismembered individual.

"It appears the penis was severed with a serrated blade of some kind. The cut is jagged. Could be from a saw, bread knife, etcetera. There weren't any fingerprints, but I did find a couple of interesting things."

"What's that?"

"There was a long, blond hair stuck on it, and I found a small fingernail chip on the glans penis."

"The what?"

"You'd call it the head."

"Why didn't you just say that then?"

"Because I'm reading from my notes."

Continuing, he said, "One side of the chip is painted red. I believe it's fingernail polish."

"Hmm, interesting. Thanks, doc. Take a look at the latest baloney pony and let me know what you find."

Doc shook his head, and I left.

When I got back to the chariot, Lucille was on the radio demanding I come back to the station. Benny Gunnerson was there and wanted to talk with me. Something about his mechanic, Walt Peterson, not showing up for work.

Lucille's a pushy broad, but she sure knows how to handle the radio. Best we've had since I came on board. She's like a mom to the department and keeps the cats and dogs in line. I gave her a 10-4, lit an Old Gold, and leaned back against the hood of the car.

It was looking like a dame was involved in this pork sword caper. I racked my brain for any lovers I'd jilted and relaxed when I couldn't think of any. At least none since Darlene Carlton back in the third grade. But that was in Texas, eight hundred miles from here, and what are the odds she even remembers my name? I hoped she didn't.

I finished my smoke and drove to the station.

Benny was standing on the steps when I pulled up. His blue, striped coveralls were spotted with grease, a red rag dangled at his rear, and a tire gauge poked out of his breast pocket.

"Benny, what can I do ya for?"

"Well, I wanna talk to you about Walt. He's my mechanic. I think you've met him before. He's been with me for a couple of years now."

"Sure, I remember him. Tall, skinny guy with kinda slouched shoulders."

"That's him."

"Come on in. Let's talk in my office."

As I passed the control room, better known as Fort Lucille, Lucille shouted, "Hey, Nolan, Lila just called in. Said they've covered a hundred yards in all directions from where the love stick was found. Didn't find anything. Wants to know what ya want 'em to do now."

The woman has a way with words. I like that about her.

"Tell them to pair up and canvass everyone within a mile of the schlong site. See if anyone saw or heard anything suspicious."

I closed my door, told Benny to sit, lit a smoke, and poured a finger of bourbon. I offered a glass to my guest, but he declined. It seems some people don't enjoy a good vice.

I stood at the window, took a sip of amber juice, and watched Mary Francis Dean arrange bouquets in front of her shop across the street. The woman with three first names. Now *there* was a classy chassis to get excited about. Too bad about the rock on her finger. Lucky Mr. Dean.

A throat cleared behind me, and I turned.

"So, Benny, talk to me about Walt."

"He didn't come to work today. That's not like him. He's never missed work before."

"Is he a drinker?"

"Well, yes, he does drink a bit. But it's never affected his work. He's never even been late before. Somethings wrong. I can feel it."

"Have you tried calling him?"

"Sure. Soon as he didn't show. Then later, I drove over to his place. Mrs. Conroy, that's his landlady, said he took off last night and never come back."

"Came."

"What?"

"Nothing. Give me her number and address, and I'll contact her if you don't hear from Walt by the end of the day."

"I don't have her number, but I'm sure it's in the book. It's Delores, Delores Conroy. She lives over on Plum Street. I don't have the exact address, but that should be listed too."

Benny left, and I walked back to the window. Unfortunately, Mary Francis had gone back inside.

There was a knock on my door, and it opened. It was Petuski. He was carrying a large envelope.

"Boss, I got the photos, and the lab didn't find any prints on the cigarette butt."

He handed me the envelope and stood there, looking like a puppy expecting a reward for not pooping on the rug.

I sat and told Petuski to do the same. He did.

The pictures didn't tell me anything I didn't

already know, except for one. I got my jeweler's loupe out and set it on the closeup of the tire print. One of the tread blocks at the edge of the tire had a jagged tear in it, and one corner of the block was missing. I showed it to Petuski.

Norb—Petuski's first name is Norbert, but I call him Norb—went back to his cubicle, and I killed the rest of the morning reviewing files and making calls.

At noon, I slipped out the back and headed across the street to Carver's Cafe for a quick lunch, hoping Mary Francis might be there. No such luck. An old couple at the back were holding hands with their heads bowed and mumbling something I couldn't make out. Probably a prayer. A businessman-type sat at the counter tearing into a burger and fries and looking like the big deal he'd hoped for didn't work out.

Paul Carver, the owner of the joint as well as cook, dishwasher, waiter, and busboy, stuck his head out from behind the grill and threw me a wave. I nodded and took a seat at the end of the counter near the window. The morning paper was on the stool next to me, so I picked it up to see what they had to say about the weenie caper from the day before. It was front-page news, and they got my name wrong again. I've told the editor before it's not Vincent, just Vince, but he's either stupid or playing with me. Five minutes later, my usual appeared: ham and cheese on rye with a side salad.

"Anything to drink today, Vince?"

"Just water."

"Comin' up."

The ham was drier than usual but edible. I was halfway through my sandwich when the door opened. I looked over and stopped chewing. A gorgeous babe with shoulder-length, blond hair stepped in. She looked my way, gave a faint smile, and sat in a booth by the wall.

I kept my jaws working but didn't take my eyes off the dame. Her lips were painted red, but she wore gloves, so I couldn't see her fingernails.

When her food arrived, she took the gloves off. I finished the last bite of my sandwich and walked by her table on my way to the restroom. Damn, if her nails weren't red.

I finished my business and motioned Paul over to the counter. "Don't look now, but do you know the blonde?"

He peeked over my shoulder, shrugged, and said, "I never saw her before."

I laid two bucks on the counter, told Paul to keep the change, walked to the alley next to Carver's, and waited for the gal to come out. She did and slipped behind the wheel of a new Dodge Coronet parked across the street. I jotted down the plate number as she drove off, then went back to the station.

Chapter 3

LILA WAS SITTING in my office when I returned from lunch. She jumped up with her cap in hand as I walked in. I sat, put my feet on the desk, and said, "Well?"

"There're six houses within a mile of the crime scene. We talked with the people at all of them but one. Nobody saw or heard anything unusual yesterday. I was told that the man we missed left a week ago to visit his daughter in Missouri. So I doubt we'll get anything from him."

"Were any of them blondes?"

"Excuse me?"

"The people you talked to; were any of them blondes?"

"Oh, no, sir."

"Thanks, Racine. Keep your ear to the ground."

"Sir?"

I looked up, raised an eyebrow, and said, "Stay alert. See what you can dig up."

"Yes, sir. Is there anything else?"

There was a lot else. But I couldn't go there and keep my job.

"Nothing at the moment. Nice work, Lila."

"Thank you, sir."

I watched her leave and wondered what she looked like out of uniform. I cut the fantasy, pulled the notepad out of my pocket, and dialed my old bowling buddy Connie "Con" Sunderson to run the blonde's plates. He supervises the local motor vehicle department and is one of the best damn bowlers in the state. Con, his wife, Ethel, my ex, Karen, and I used to bowl every Wednesday and Saturday for the first three years we lived in Rockland. Con and I still enjoy a drink on occasion. He picked up on the third ring.

"Sunderson."

"Constance, it's Vince."

"Mr. Nolan, how're they hangin'?"

"Low. I need a favor."

"Sure. What's up?"

"I need you to run a plate for me."

"Hit me."

"193BAB."

"Got it. That all?"

"That's it for now."

"I'll run it and get back at ya."

"Thanks, buddy."

I dialed Doc Williams to get the lowdown on the pork sword I dropped off earlier.

"Doctor Williams."

"Doc, it's Vince. What have you got on the latest detached dingy?"

"Do you ever call it by its correct name?"

"Not unless I have to."

"Well, suit yourself. The blood on the penis is B negative, and it looks like it was severed with the same serrated blade as the first. B negative is rare. It's only found in about two percent of the population. That's all I've got for you."

"Thanks, Doc. That helps a lot. It looks like

the two are definitely connected—or were."

I hung up, spread the pictures from both crime scenes on my desk, and ran a nose rag over my cheaters. I didn't use to need the damn things, but about two years ago, I realized I couldn't hold the paper out any farther and still be in the same room to read it. Whoever said the best is yet to come either wasn't farsighted or never learned to read. I was making a second pass over the photos when the phone rang.

"Nolan."

"Vince, I pulled the tags. Here's what I've got. You ready?"

"Shoot."

"The car's registered to a Christine Martin from Douglas County. The other end of the state. It's a 1954 Dodge Coronet and hasn't been reported stollen. The last address is 2378 Pine Tree Lane in Centerville. No phone number listed, but it should be in the Centerville book if she's got one."

"Thanks, Connie. I owe ya one."

"No, you owe me two. I never got a beer for the last one I pulled, you cheapskate."

"Bye, Constance."

I figured there was no point in trying to ring her now since she wasn't in Centerville. That would have to wait. Maybe I'd get lucky and run into her again if she was still in town.

I finished going over the pictures and starting to nod off from lack of sleep. I kicked off my shoes, put my feet up, leaned my chair back, and nodded off.

The curtains were drawn, but the hazy light

from a streetlight found its way through and sil-houetted a pair of gams standing at the end of the bed. The negligee they were holding up looked inviting. The gams started moving closer as the negligee floated to the floor. A blonde with bright red lips sat on the bed and put her lips close to mine.

RING ... RING.

It was the damn phone. My head flew up, and the dame was gone. I fumbled for the phone and tried to sound alert.

"Nolan."

"You sound sleepy. Did I wake you?"

I cleared my throat and said, "Who is this?"

"It's me, Benny, from the garage."

"Oh, yeah, Benny. What's up?"

"I'm closing up for the day and wanted to let you know that I never heard from Walt. Something is wrong for sure."

"OK, Benny. Thanks. I'll track down Mrs. Conroy and see what she knows."

I hung up and noticed it was getting dark out. Petuski was still jabbering away at his desk. I lit a smoke and found the Plum Street address in the book. I wanted silence on the way to see Mrs. Conroy, so I grabbed my hat off the rack and snuck out the side door.

Chapter 4

THE STREET LIGHTS popped on when I pulled out of the station. It was a gray night, and drizzle started dancing across the windshield. I turned on the wipers and made a left. Delores Conroy lived on the west side, just before town turned to country.

I pulled to the curb in front of her place and killed the engine. It was an old Victorian with great bones that could have been on the cover of *Better Homes and Gardens*. The broad had money.

A rich-sounding chime oozed through the door when I hit the doorbell. I liked the sound and pushed it again. That brought a "Coming" from Mrs. Conroy.

She opened the door and was everything I imagined Mrs. Santa Claus would look like, including a pair of round, wire-rimmed glasses. Although, I didn't picture Santa's wife with blue-tinted hair.

"Yes?"

"Mrs. Conroy?"

"Yes."

"I'm Detective Nolan with Rockland PD."

"Oh, I thought I'd be hearing from you ever since Benny came around looking for Walter. Did something happen to him?"

"Not that I know of ma'am. Just trying to find him."

She stepped back and said, "Please, do come in."

"Thank you, ma'am."

She showed me to the parlor and sat in a floral-patterned overstuffed chair next to the fireplace. The flames were high, and the slight scent of burning wood permeated the room. It was chilly out, and the heat felt good. I sat on a matching sofa across from her.

"Before we start, Detective, would you care for coffee?"

"Thank you, no. It keeps me up if I drink it late."

"Bourbon?"

I was beginning to like this dame. "Sure."

"Sit tight. I'll be right back." She stood, turned, and said, "You look like a man who likes it straight. Am I right?"

I assumed she was talking about the bourbon and said, "Bingo."

"I knew it. That's how my Harold liked it. I do too."

She left the room trailed by a hint of lavender. A classy old girl.

I scoped out the room and saw a silver-framed photo of an attractive young couple on the mantel. I stood to take a closer look.

The old lady returned, carrying two crystal tumblers, both with a hefty pour. I could be friends with this one.

She handed me a glass, took a sip from the other one, and said, "Please, sit."

I took a sizeable swallow and accepted her offer.

"Mrs. Conroy—"

"Delores, please."

"Delores, how long have you known Walt Peterson?"

"Ever since he moved back to Rockland, about two years now. He rented my upstairs the day he got here. He's such a nice young man. Always helps around the place. He does most of the yard work, painted the garage, and replaced the starter on my car. I give him a break on the rent because he helps me so much. He grew up here, you know?"

"No. I didn't know that. Is he a drinker?"

"Oh, we share a drink now and then. But I've never known it to be a problem. Why, have you heard something?"

"No, ma'am. Just asking."

"I'm so worried that he didn't go to work today. I haven't seen him since he left last night."

"What can you tell me about last night?"

"Well, let's see. He left about seven with some woman I'd not seen before. That was unusual because I've never seen Walt with a woman."

"Can you tell me what she looked like?"

"Walter has his own entrance, so I don't usually know his comings and goings. I heard him talking with a woman as they walked down the side of the house. That got my curiosity up, so I watched from the front window. It was dark, and I couldn't see much. Her car was parked under the streetlight, so I saw she had blond hair and was almost as tall as Walter, and he must be six feet if he's an inch. I'd guess her at five-ten."

"You're sure she was blonde?"

"Oh, yes."

"How long was her hair?"

"I don't know. The collar of her coat was turned up, and her hair was tucked inside."

"Do you know where they went?"

"I have no idea. Walter never said anything about going out."

"Do you remember what kind of car it was?"

"On, dear, I'm not very good with cars. It was big. There were four doors, I know that, for sure. I don't know the make because they all look the same to me."

"How about the color?"

"Like I said, it was dark out, but I remember it was a light color, maybe light gray or green. I'm not sure."

"Delores, you've been most helpful."

I stood, drained the last of the bourbon, and handed her my card.

"Please, give me a call if you hear from Walt or can think of anything else that might help."

"I will, Detective."

She walked me to the door, and I thanked her again for the bourbon. Her eyes locked on mine for a moment, and I sensed a longing I wasn't about to do anything about. I was still a few years away from liver spots and sagging skin.

I pulled a U-ey and backtracked through town to my place. I needed sleep, especially after the hypnotic effect of the fireplace and a double shot of bourbon.

Petuski's car was still in the lot when I drove past the station, and I could see him through the window, still yakking on the horn. I hoped it was business but doubted it. For a twenty-five-year-old man, the guy has a lot of teenage girl in him.

There were several cars parked outside the Hideaway Lounge. It was always busy, even mid-week, and tonight was no exception. Nice place, but not my style; too many suits and tablecloths. I prefer sawdust and dartboards.

I glanced over and thought I saw the trunk end of a new Dodge Coronet parked at the back of the lot. I hit the brakes, threw my ride into reverse, and pulled into the lot. What do you know? The plate number was 193BAB.

There was a parking spot open on the street next to the lounge, so I backed out and parked. I walked back to the Dodge to have a look around. My flashlight battery was getting low but put out enough light to see inside the car. There was nothing in the car to indicate that Blondie was our chode chopper. I couldn't see under the tires, but none of the visible tread blocks were torn or missing a corner. I walked to the sidewalk and entered the joint.

The usual look-at-me-aren't-I-impressive crowd was there, doing their deals and sipping wine with their pinkies extended. God help me if I'm ever in here except on business.

The babe I was looking for was sitting alone at the end of the bar, smoking a cig, and sipping from a cone-shaped glass of clear liquid with three olives stuck on a little plastic sword. I guessed martini.

I grabbed a stool at the end of the bar near the door with a clear view of Blondie. I ordered my usual, Jim Beam Black, no ice. The bartender set my drink on an expensive-looking coaster, threw me a thin smile, and sashayed back to the honey he was hitting on. He could tell this wasn't my kind of place. Maybe it was the frayed suit or the tobacco drool stain on my shoulder that tipped him off. I didn't care.

I tossed the last of my drink down my throat and was about to order another when a stud got up from the table where he'd been talking way too loud with his buddies and strolled over to Blondie. He stood with his back to me and blocked my view of the action. Blondie let out a girlie giggle, and the cat went back to his table.

I played with my empty glass while scoping out the action. Laughter erupted from Casanova's table. He got up, glanced at the blonde, and left. Two minutes later, Blondie put her smokes in her purse, picked up her keys from the bar, and walked out. I couldn't help but notice how stiletto heels and the tight dress made her posterior roll like ocean waves. I kind of hoped she wasn't our suspect.

I grabbed my hat and threw seventy-five cents on the bar. I figured drinks were more expensive here than at the Rusty Nail, my favorite dive bar, and I didn't care if there was enough for a tip. The barkeep's snooty smile nixed any possibility of a monetary reward. I thought about taking back one of the quarters but hurried out before Miss Christine could get away.

The temperature had dropped several degrees since I entered the joint, and a cold blast of October air gave me a slap when I hit the street. I looked left and right but didn't see anyone. It was quiet. Maybe they'd gone to Christine's car for a game of back seat bingo. I started for the lot when car lights came on, and an engine came to life half a block behind me. I assumed it was Casanova, so I hightailed it to my car to wait and see if the blonde pulled out. She did and began to follow the other car. I waited until she was a block away before tailing her.

Three blocks down, the car she was following made a left. Blondie kept going straight. She made a left on ninth, a right on Dickerson, and pulled into the driveway of a respectable pad with a realtor's sold sign in front. I pulled over as she got out and went into the house.

I staked the place out for an hour to see if she'd leave or the flutter bum from the lounge would show. Neither happened, and her place went dark at 9:10.

I needed to visit the sandman, so I fired up the Ford and headed home.

Chapter 5

I WOKE AT seven to the sound of the bone-head next door revving his Harley and riding off to work. The bed was warm, and I was in no hurry to dive back into the dingus disaster. I scratched my belly, picked lint from my navel, and watched a robin wrestle an earthworm outside my window.

My apartment was cold, and I kicked up the heat on my way to the kitchen. The Folger's coffee can was sitting on the counter where I'd left it the day before. I shook it and didn't like the sound it made. There weren't enough grounds to make a cup, so I eighty-sixed it. Fortunately, yesterday's grounds were still in the filter. I added water to the percolator, hit the switch, and hoped for the best. The result was light-brown, tasteless water.

I found a pack of Old Golds under the bed, lit one, and watched the robin, who was now in a tug-of-war with its mate over the worm. I rooted for the early bird that found it.

My last pair of boxers reminded me that I'd either have to do laundry soon or turn them inside out and go for a second round. I nosed the pits of the shirt I wore yesterday, and getting a slight hint of Old Spice, put it on. My frayed suit and fedora rounded out the ensemble.

I opened the door with an eye out for the fur ball that was intent on moving in. It was nowhere in sight. I stepped out, did a couple of side twists to get the kink out of my back, and walked to the car.

When I got to the office, a copy of yesterday's *Rockland Gazette* was on my desk. A large picture of Racine, Petuski, two other uniforms, and me was plastered across the top of the front page. We were staring down at a patch of grass. The headline in extra-large print screamed SECOND SEVERED MALE PENIS FOUND. The inclusion of the term *male* was beyond over-kill, but, hey, it's a small-town rag and the work of an over-zealous cub reporter.

Petuski talked with the reporter yesterday and had given her the information we wanted to get out. The article mentioned the long blond hair and indicated a woman might be involved. It asked anyone with information to please contact Detective Vince Nolan at the Rockland PD.

My phone rang.

"Nolan."

"Detective Nolan?"

"Speaking."

"Oh good. Detective, this is Imogene Strickland. You don't know me, but I've lived here in Rockland my whole life. I read in the paper about the, uh, thing you found, and I think my neighbor did it."

"Who's your neighbor?"

"Doris DeWalt."

"And why do you think Doris did it?"

"Well, she's got long blond hair."

"That it?"

"Oh, goodness, no. There's more. She's just

plain nasty, and she hates men."

"I see. How is she nasty?"

"You should hear the things she says to my Albert. It's downright disrespectful. Why the other day, Albert went out to get the paper, and Doris was sitting out on her porch. Albie, that's what I call him, said good evening to her, and she gave him the nastiest look I'd ever seen and said something that sounded like 'Who says.' Can you imagine?"

"No ma'am, that's pretty hard to believe. What else can you tell me about nasty Doris?"

"She's had cerebral palsy since she was born. She must be forty and still lives with her parents, can you believe that?"

I said, "Yes, ma'am, I can. Thank you for calling," and hung up. The number of idiots that populate this earth has always amazed me.

There was a knock at my door, and Petuski walked in.

"Morning, boss."

I shot him my don't-call-me-boss look and said, "Petuski ... aw, forget it. Let's take a drive and have another look-see around the park where the first pecker was found."

"OK."

The smell of coffee caught my attention as we passed the breakroom. I poured a cup, burned my tongue, and dumped it. It was the dregs of the morning's first pot and tasted like burnt mud.

I glanced in Fort Lucille. Lucille was busy handling radio chatter but not too busy to give me a middle-digit salute. I gave her a chin flick and moved on.

The breeze from the north had died, and it was a lot warmer than yesterday. Typical October weather. I tossed my suit coat on the back seat and fired the engine.

Petuski was quiet for the first five minutes. His lips curved in a stupid grin, and he seemed lost in space. I could tell he had something on his mind.

"What is it, Norb?"

He snapped back to the moment. "Huh?"

"You're quiet. What is it?"

"Oh, just thinking."

"About?"

"Last night. Thinking about last night."

I made the mistake of continuing and said, "What about it?"

The stupid grin blossomed into a face-splitting smile, and he said, "Me and Lila met for drinks last night."

I hit the brakes and skidded to a stop on the side of the road. Petuski grabbed the dash with both hands, and the smile turned to a look of terror.

"Petuski, damn it. Where did you go to school?"

He opened his mouth to talk, but I cut him off.

"Did you take grammar?"

He nodded.

"Well, you could fool me. How many times do I have to tell you that when you're talking about another person and you doing something together, you always start with the other person and then break down the sentence like each of you is doing the thing alone."

He opened his mouth again, and I cut him off again.

"So, in *your* sentence, you say Lila's name first. You'd say Lila met for drinks last night. Got it?"

He nodded.

"Then ask yourself if the term *me* is correct. Does it sound right to you to say me met for drinks last night?"

He continued to stare at me, slack-jawed.

"No, it doesn't. Does, I met for drinks last night sound correct to you?"

He bobbed his head.

"Good boy. So now you say Lila and I met for drinks last night. Can you do that?"

"Uh-huh."

There wasn't a peep from Norb the rest of the drive. It was a nice change from his usual chatter. He stared straight ahead with a puzzled look etched on his mug. I had hopes that the guy would get it one day. How he made it through the academy is beyond me. Standards must have dropped since I was a recruit.

Shady Rock Park was just off Route 14, less than a mile from where the second baloney pony was found. I wondered how the perp was connected to this stretch of highway. Or was there a connection? Maybe it was simply happenstance.

The park was still closed. I rolled to a stop outside the gate and got out. Petuski had recovered from his roadside grammar lesson and followed.

Norb and I split up and combed the area for twenty yards in all directions from where the first penis was found. Nothing. We were walking back to the car when I stopped.

"What is it, boss?"

"Go on back. I'll be right there."

He went to the car, and I went back to the spot next to the picnic table where the remnant of manhood had been tossed. I had a knot in my gut that told me I was missing something. But what?

I stood still and slowly examined an imaginary grid surrounding the area. I didn't see anything unusual. I started at the top of the grid again and worked my way down. Halfway through the grid, I saw it. Barely visible, but it was there. A wooden matchstick with only the tip sticking out from under a leaf. Could the perp have dropped it? It was a picnic area, so lots of people could have dropped it. But it was late October and had been too cold for people to have been eating in the park. And we had heavy rain a week ago. This match looked like it hadn't been there long.

I waved at Petuski and told him to bring the camera. He snapped a couple of pictures and went back to the car. I put on gloves and put the stick in a bag.

Tim Collins is Rockland PD's lab cop. The kid has a bachelor's in chemistry with a master's in human biology. Why he chose Rockland to ply his trade is anybody's guess. But I'm glad we have him. I once asked him if he had a brother named Tom. And in true nerd fashion, he looked at me with a straight face and said, "No, I don't have any siblings."

Collins's lab is in a corner of the station basement. The old wooden stairs creaked as I stepped down to his office. I wondered how any human being could stand to work in such a tomb. The floor and walls were drab concrete, the ceiling beams were laced with cobwebs from spiders long dead, and two small, grimy windows near the ceiling provided the only natural light. But Collins seemed content with his microscope, slides, and solutions.

"Collins. Got a minute?"

He banged his head on the suspended lampshade as he jerked up from the slide he was studying.

"Oh, Detective, hi. Sure. What's up?"

I laid the bag with the matchstick on the lab table and said, "I found a wooden match at the first crime scene. I want you to check it out and let me know what you find."

"I'll get on it as soon as I'm finished with this slide."

"Thanks, Collins."

I looked around at the dreary surroundings, shook my head, and creaked back up the stairs.

There was a note on my desk when I got back to my office. It was in Lucille's chicken scratch.

CALL ROSEMARY ANDERSON
SOUNDS URGENT 273-9842

Rosemary Anderson. The name sounded familiar, but I didn't know why.

The wall clock showed 9:30, time for a mid-morning pick-me-up. I unlocked my desk drawer, pulled out my friend Mr. Beam, and poured a couple of fingers. The Old Golds beckoned me, so I lit one, grabbed my glass, and stood at the window, hoping to catch a glimpse of Mary Francis. It wasn't in the cards.

Chapter 6

THE PHONE RANG six times, and I was about to hang up when a grating voice answered.

"Hello."

"Mrs. Anderson?"

"Yes."

"It's Detective Nolan."

"Detective. Oh, thank you for calling. Detective, I'm worried sick about my Mason."

"Why's that?"

"Well, he always calls me every evening when he's out of town. He sells encyclopedias, and his territory is the eastern half of the state. So, he's usually away one or two nights a week."

Her high-pitched screeching made me want to hang up. I figured Mason was on a beach somewhere in Mexico, thankful to not be waking up to it every morning.

"When did you last hear from your husband?"

"Three days ago. He left late in the afternoon on Tuesday. Said he wanted to get to Lakefield so he could get an early start the next morning. Lakefield's a hundred fifty miles west of here."

"Yes, ma'am. I know where Lakefield is."

"He called me and said he'd made it. That was the last time I heard from him."

"What time did he call?"

"Eight o'clock. I know it was eight because that's when he always calls. After he's had his evening shower, and I put Muffy out."

"Muffy?"

"My Pomeranian. She always goes out at eight to do her last business of the day."

"Hmm. Has your husband ever not called before when he was out of town?"

"Never. Well, let me see, there was the one time a few years back when a storm took out the phone line. But he called first thing the next morning when it was repaired."

I held the phone away from my ear to deaden the piercing prattle and said, "Uh-huh."

"I'm so worried, Detective, especially after reading about what has been happening to men here in town."

I took down her husband's information, tried to reassure her that he was probably alright, and hung up, thankful for the silence. But I couldn't help wondering if Mason, wherever he was, might be a couple of pounds lighter than when he left home.

The stack of files on my desk kept me occupied until hunger reminded me it was time for lunch. The combination of alcohol, bad coffee, cigarettes, and no breakfast was making my gut rumble like my neighbor's Harley. I was reaching for my coat when Collins walked in.

"Vince, we got a break on the match you found."

I turned, not happy about the interruption to my lunch plans, and pointed to a chair. Collins sat.

"What you got?"

"Talk about a coincidence. I got my matches out to light the Bunsen burner when I saw the similarity. They looked a lot like the match you found, so I studied them under the microscope. Bingo!"

His goofy ear-to-ear smile exposed the gap in his front teeth and caused his cheeks to puff out, pushing freckles closer to his eyes. The Alfred E. Neuman likeness made me laugh.

"Sir?"

"Nothing. Go on."

"Well, your match and my match, match. They're both one and a half inches long, they have the same hexagonal shape to the stick, and are tipped with the same white sulfur. And the wood is the same color. The hexagonal shape is very unusual. Most are square."

"Where did you get your matches?"

"At Dexter's Grill over on third. I'm a hamburger nut, and Dexter's has the best burgers around, in my opinion. I eat lunch there every Wednesday, come rain or shine, and I always pick up a box. They're those little promotional boxes with twenty-five matches and the Dexter's Grill name printed on the box."

"That should narrow down our list of potential suspects. There can't be more than a thousand of those boxes floating around town."

"That's true. But it's another piece of the puzzle. Oh, and I almost forgot. There's a small dot of red on the stick that's the same color as the lipstick on the cigarette butt you gave me yesterday. She must have stuck it in her mouth for some reason."

Now that got my attention. "Good work, Collins. That helps a lot."

The goofy smile returned as he said, "Thank you, sir," and backed out of my office.

I decided to shake up my routine and drove to Dexter's Grill for lunch. Collins made the burgers sound pretty good, and I wanted to talk to the staff.

Dexter's is a nondescript joint wedged between a beauty parlor and a dress shop. DEX ER'S GRILL was painted in gold on the front window. The *T* had been scratched off long ago, and the rest of the letters were alligatored. An equally worn OPEN sign was tapped in a lower corner of the window. I'd have never gone in without Collins's recommendation.

The place was warm and smelled of grease. I sat at a table near the window and wiped crumbs from the last burger fanatic onto the floor. I flipped through the menu and decided on the classic with a side of fries.

A pasty stick of a woman appeared at my table with a pen in one hand and an order pad in the other. Her gray hair was whipped up into a bird's nest on top of her head, and the bags under her eyes cried for sleep.

Her smoker's voice said, "Can I take your order?"

I assumed she was able to take my order but wasn't sure I wanted her to. She was all business, no unnecessary chatter, which suited me fine.

"Give me the classic and a side of fries."

"How do you want it?"

"On a plate will be fine."

The wrinkles around her mouth stretched into a slight smile.

"You know what I mean, smartass."

It must have been years since she'd been voted waitress of the month, if ever.

"Burn it."

"Anything else?"

"Nope."

She left to put my order on the wheel, and I caught a whiff of cheap perfume and body odor. I considered walking out when I noticed the table-top jukebox. It was the only redeeming thing I'd noticed about the place. It held one hundred songs, and you could play three of them for a nickel.

I flipped through the playlist, dropped in a nickel, and punched the buttons for my selections: "Young at Heart" by Frank Sinatra, "Mr. Sandman" by the Chordettes, and "Sh'boom (Life Could be a Dream)" by the Chords. I wondered if the Chords were The Chordettes' brothers.

I lit a smoke and stared out the window, listening to the tunes. My mind wandered to my ex, Karen, and the time we made love in the sand out at Travis Lake while listening to Frank croon. Damn, she was good. What in the hell happened? Things were sweet at first. I guess my dedication to the job wore on her, that and her affair with her old college flame, Matt Heideger.

The clatter of a plate and silverware ended my trip down memory lane. Just as well. Stick woman and her odor were back without fanfare. She slapped the check on the table and disappeared without a word.

The burger was OK, but I didn't experience Collins's "burgerphoria." The fries, on the other hand, were exceptional. I thought about getting a second order but figured I'd reached my grease quota for the day.

I took the check to the register and waited for Miss Congeniality to ring me up. She was at the end of the counter, marrying ketchup bottles.

Without looking up, she said, "Hold your horses."

She was lucky I didn't own the joint.

When the marriage concluded, she sauntered to the register and grabbed the two quarters I'd laid on the counter. The bill was forty cents. She held onto my change as she glanced at the table where I'd been sitting. Not seeing a tip, she slapped the dime on the counter, made an unintelligible grunt, and returned to her marriage duties.

I said, "Excuse me," and motioned for her to come back. She did, which surprised me.

"Yeah?"

"Have you seen a blond woman in here over the past few months, a smoker, perhaps wearing bright red lipstick and nail polish?"

"Nope. Why, you lookin' for some action?"

I ignored her question and said, "How about someone driving a new, blue Dodge Coronet?"

"Nope."

"You're sure?"

"Yup."

"Is Dexter here?"

The old bitty pursed her lips and threw a

hand in the direction of the grill man.

The head floating above the grill counter was round, topped with a white sailor's cap, and sporting a red, bulbous nose, the likes of which I'd never seen before.

I moved to the grill and said, "Dexter?"

The head lifted and said, "Yeah."

I held up my badge and said, "Got a minute?"

His squinty eyes grew wide, ash dropped from his cigarette, and he said, "Give me a minute."

I took a seat at the counter in front of the grill and waited. A couple of minutes later, a plate was laid on the grill counter, and the ding of a bell alerted dingbat that her order was ready. Dexter appeared from behind the grill, sporting a belly that complimented his nose.

"Yeah?"

"Dexter, I'm Detective Nolan. I'd like to ask you a couple of questions."

"Yeah."

Given his personality, I was beginning to see how Miss Congeniality kept her job. They were cut from the same swatch of stained cloth.

I asked him the same questions, and the only person he could think of that matched my query was an old gal who'd been coming in for years. She had short, dyed-blond hair and was in her late eighties. He didn't recall ever seeing her with lipstick or nail polish.

I thanked Dexter and left, hoping to never return.

Chapter 7

PETUSKI WAS WAITING for me in the lobby when I got back to the station.

"Boss, we got a call from Emma Carlson about ten minutes ago. She runs the Starlight Motel over in Valley. She says a Floyd Benson checked in on Tuesday evening and hasn't been seen since. His car's still there, but there's no sign of him. She's worried because of what she read in the paper about the penises."

I knew the Starlight because of some prostitution activity that took place there a few years ago. It's a twelve-unit dive that stays afloat thanks to unsuspecting summer tourists who want a cheap place to crash for the night.

I was out of smokes, so I told Petuski to wait and headed to the break room. I searched my pockets for a quarter, and coming up empty, bummed one from Lucille.

"That's two this week, Nolan. I'm writing 'em down."

I gave her a raised-arm salute, clicked my heels, and said, "Thanks, gorgeous."

I dropped the quarter in the machine and pulled the lever. Nothing. The damn thing was a relic from the days when cops rode horses. I rocked it back and forth a couple of times before the Old Golds gave up and dropped.

Valley is a dreary little collection of rundown houses, a small market, and the Starlight. It's a bedroom community for the unskilled workers of Rockland.

The first thing I noticed when we pulled into the Starlight was a black 1953 Chevrolet Bel-Air. It was the only car there and was parked in front of room 12, the farthest room from the office. I assumed it belonged to our reason for coming to this godforsaken backwater.

The smell of liver and onions greeted us when we entered the lobby. There was no one in sight, so I hit the bell next to the cash register.

"Just a minute."

I looked around and wondered why anyone in their right mind would book a room after seeing the lobby. In addition to the stink of the worst meal ever concocted, the sofa seats were shedding stuffing, a dead plant of some sort graced the window, and brochures shouting the wonders of the area were scattered on the floor.

A woman waddled through the door separating the lobby from the living space. She was a perfect match for the lobby. Gray hair was plastered to her head, oversized pink glasses made her eyes bug out, her chins jiggled from side to side as she walked, and her tent-sized muumuu had a stain the size of Texas over her left boob. The sight of that woman alone would make me get back in the car and look for lodging elsewhere.

I said, "Miss Carlson?"

"You're lookin' at her."

Yes, I was, all of her.

"I'm Detective Nolan, and this is Detective Petuski. You called about a Floyd Benson."

"I sure did. I don't know what's going on with that man, but his car hasn't moved since he checked in on Tuesday, and I haven't seen him around."

"What time did he check in on Tuesday?"

She pulled a registration card from the file and said, "It's wrote right here. Six fifty-three."

"Written."

"What?"

"Nothing. Was anyone with him?"

"Not that I seen."

I rolled my eyes and continued. "What else can you tell us?"

"The do not disturb sign has been on the door since he got here. He paid for one night but rang the office about nine on Tuesday and said he'd be staying awhile longer. I went over a couple of times today to see about payment, but he never come to the door. That's why I called you guys."

I said, "Grab the keys to number twelve. Let's have a look."

It was a cool day, but Emma's breath came hard, and she broke a sweat as she made her way to unit twelve.

I knocked. No response. I knocked again and said, "Mr. Benson, open up, it's the police. I'd like to have a word with you." Still no response.

I tried the door, but it was locked. Petuski and I drew our guns. I looked at the wheezing lump of flesh standing next to me and said, "Open it."

Emma's hand was shaking and sweat dotted her upper lip as she inserted the key. She unlocked the door then got behind me, pressing her mass against the building wall.

Petuski looked nervous. It was the first time he'd drawn his weapon outside of the range. I did a silent three count raising one finger at a time, then pushed the door open and entered with my Colt Detective Special at the ready. Emma gave a high-pitched squeal as Petuski followed me in.

The bathroom door was closed. I moved toward it as Petuski checked the closet. Both were empty.

The bed was a mess, and there was a large spot of blood on the bottom sheet. A set of keys was on the floor next to the bed. Other than that, there was nothing to indicate anyone had been in the room.

Petuski got his camera to photograph the evidence while I radioed for the tow truck and for Collins to come out and inspect the scene.

The Bel-Air was unlocked, so I put on gloves and opened the door. The ashtray was pulled out and filled with non-filtered cigarette butts. A pair of tan driving gloves lay on the passenger seat. I opened the glove box and found a map of the state, a half-full bottle of cheap whiskey, and surprise, surprise, a registration card bearing the name Mason Anderson. A suitcase containing men's clothes lay on the back seat. Next to it was a large, black bag filled with *Encyclopedia Britannica* brochures and sample books. I was pretty certain at this point that even if Anderson were found alive, his days of doing the mattress mambo were over.

Collins showed up twenty minutes after I'd

called, and the tow truck was right behind him. He dusted the room for prints and pulled several from the phone, doorknobs, nightstand, and television. A close examination of the bed turned up a blond hair on the pillow that was about the same length as the one Doc Williams found. Collins bagged the hair, keys, and sheet and went back to his lab.

Petuski and I helped the tow truck driver push the car back so he could get the tow chains hooked up and move the car to the impound lot where Collins could give it a thorough going-over.

Emma was still standing in front of unit 12, watching the work. I had her lock up and told her no one was to go into the room until I gave her the OK. She didn't look happy but nodded.

Norb and I started for the car when Emma shouted, "Hey." We both turned to see muumuu mama with her feet spread, hands on her hips, and a determined look on her mug.

I said, "Yes?"

"Well, who's gonna pay for it?"

"Excuse me?"

"The sheet. Who's gonna pay for it?"

"Ma'am, this is a criminal investigation. The sheet is your contribution to solving it."

"That ain't right."

I said, "Take it up with the mayor," and continued to the car.

Norb and I both let out a chuckle.

"I heard that."

I gave her a wave without looking back and drove back to Rockland.

Chapter 8

WE WERE PASSING near the Anderson place on our way to the station, so I pulled off the highway and headed in that direction.

Petuski looked at me and said, "Where are we going?"

"Anderson's place. We've got to tell Mrs. Anderson what we found and get something with Anderson's prints on it to compare with the prints from the motel and car."

"Oh, jeez, what do we tell her?"

"Just what we found."

"Have you done this before, tell someone something bad may have happened to their spouse?"

"Unfortunately, yes. It's my least favorite part of the job. You never really get used to it."

A panicked look spread across Mrs. Anderson's face when she saw us. Her lower lip quivered, and she said, "Oh, no, officers. Where's my Mason?"

Petuski was frozen, too afraid to speak.

"We don't know, ma'am. Can we talk inside?"

"Yes, please come in."

She stepped back and grabbed the doorknob to steady herself. We took seats in the living room as Mrs. Anderson pulled a hanky out of her dress pocket and wiped tears from her eyes. Mascara streaked her cheeks, and her sobs grew louder as I explained what we'd found.

"But you must be wrong. Mason went to Lakefield. He called me from there Tuesday evening. I told you that."

"Yes, ma'am, you did. But the registration log shows that he checked into the motel on Tuesday evening. I'm sorry. Do you have any idea why he did that?"

"No. Mason has never lied to me."

"Ma'am, we'd like to get something of Mason's with his fingerprints on it, so we can compare his prints to the ones found at the motel and on the car."

She took a moment to fight back the tears and said, "Of course. His drinking glass is next to the bed. He always keeps water next to the bed in case he gets thirsty during the night. I'll get it."

"Wait, ma'am. Let me get it. We don't want to contaminate it with other prints."

"Of course, I forgot."

She stood and led me into the bedroom. I put on gloves and secured the glass in an evidence bag. I asked Mrs. Anderson to come to the station to provide her prints. She agreed and said she'd be there within the hour.

Petuski and I thanked her and assured her that we'd let her know if we found out anything more about her husband.

A very shaken Rosemary Anderson watched through the screen door as Petuski and I stepped off the porch and drove away.

Back at the station, Norb went to the darkroom to process the motel pictures. I dropped Anderson's water glass off with Collins and told him Mrs. Anderson was on her way in, then headed to my office to confer with my friend Mr. Beam. I passed Lila's desk on the way and stopped.

"So, Miss Racine, how was your date with Norb?"

She looked up, confused. "What?"

"Your date with Norb last night. He said you met for drinks."

"Oh, my God, you've got to be kidding me."

"I'm not."

"I didn't go out with Norb last night. I met some of the guys for a drink after work, and he walked in and sat at our table. I didn't even talk to the guy. He sat there for ten minutes, didn't order anything, and left."

"I guess he considers that a date."

She rolled her eyes and went back to work.

I closed my office door, lit a smoke, and had just gotten Mr. Beam's cap off when the phone rang. It was Collins.

"Vince, I just finished typing the blood on the sheet from the motel. It's type O positive, same as on the first penis. And the hair matches the hair Doc Williams found. It's got the same attributes, including pigment distribution and scale patterns."

"Thanks, Collins. Looks like Rosemary Anderson won't be enjoying the old bump and grind anymore. At least not with her Mason."

"Sir?"

"Rosemary's the wife of the man who was attached to the first meat puppet we found."

There was silence on the other end of the line.

"Listen, Collins. The car was towed to the impound lot. Check it out and let me know what you find."

He sounded distant when he said, "Yeah, sure, I'll get on it first thing in the morning."

I hung up and screwed my friend's cap back on. It was getting late, and I'd had enough of the trouser monkey conundrum for one day. The Rusty Nail, my home away from home, was calling. A visit to the Nail was my favorite way to end the day.

A blue haze hung over the bar, and the crack of a cue ball echoed from the back room when I walked in the joint. I took my regular seat at the bar and set my fedora on the stool next to me. Hank Williams's "Cold Cold Heart" was playing on the jukebox, and it took me back to the last fight I had with Karen. I'd gotten home late and went to give her a kiss when the scent of English Leather stopped me. I didn't wear English Leather. I hated the smell and thought only sissies wore it. It turns out Karen had spent the day with her old flame, Matt Heideger. We went at it for an hour before I slammed the door on my way out. I spent the night in my car and never went back except to get my things.

I must have been lost in Sadville for quite awhile because, suddenly, there were four empty double shots of whiskey staring at me. I hadn't eaten since Dexter's and was feeling the booze. Three drunk broads screaming along with Darrell Glenn and his hit single, "Crying In The Chapel," was enough to get my butt out of there.

The cold night air slapped some clarity on my foggy mind as I stepped onto the sidewalk. My car was right there, but I wasn't in the best driving condition. I decided to walk. My pad was only seven blocks away, and the walk would do me good.

I'd gone a couple of blocks when a blue 1954 Dodge Coronet pulled up beside me. The driver's window rolled down, and a smiling Christine Martin was looking at me. I felt my manhood shrivel as I wondered if she could be the wang wacker.

"Evening, Detective. Need a ride?"

I didn't but figured it was a chance to learn more about her.

"Sure."

"Hop in."

The chill air caused my breath to vaporize as I walked around the car and got in. The heater was turned on high, and it felt good.

She stuck out a gloved hand and said, "I'm Christine, but you already know that."

"I do?"

"You do. Paul Carver told me you asked about me."

"Hmm."

I made a mental note to talk to Carver about the meaning of confidentiality.

"I saw you watching me yesterday at the cafe and again at the Hideaway, so I asked Paul about you at lunch today. He's quite a talker."

"I see."

"Oh, and your surveillance skills need work. I saw you waiting for me in the alley outside Carver's and later parked outside my house."

She gave me a flirtatious smile, put the car in

gear, and hit the gas.

Who is this dame? I have to admit, I was impressed.

"So, Miss Martin, what's your story?"

"I just moved here from Centerville. But I'm sure you already know that too. I received my degree in forensic science from NYU and worked as a forensics officer with the NYPD for fifteen years before burning out and moving to Centerville."

She caught me looking at her and said, "Surprised?"

"Yeah."

"Retirement bored me, so I applied for the forensics position at Rockland J C and got it. I start classes in January."

As she was talking, I noticed a blond hair on the seatback next to her. I rested my arm on the seatback and collected the hair between my thumb and index finger. She pulled up in front of my building and stopped. I thanked her for the ride and got out. I started to walk away when the window rolled down.

"By the way, Vince, the hair won't match."

I turned and said, "Excuse me?"

"The hair you just picked up. It won't match the hair found at the crime scene."

She threw me a cocky smile and drove off. I watched the car until it turned and disappeared. Blondie was good. I hoped she was right about the hair.

The door lock to my apartment was old and had a mind of its own. It liked to stick, especially when it was cold. I had to jiggle the key several times before it finally gave up and let me in. I was almost sorry it did. The place was cold and smelled of garbage that should have been taken out days ago.

I flicked on the light and made a beeline to the floor heater. I removed the floor grate and went through the tricky routine of lighting the pilot and kicking on the heat. I replaced the grate and stood over it, letting the heat work its way up my pant legs.

A rumbling in my stomach moved me off the grate and into the kitchen, where a search of the fridge and cupboard reminded me grocery shopping day had long passed. I cut a spot of mold off a slice of bread and dropped it in the toaster. I found my last can of tomato soup, and when the toast popped up, I put the toast in a bowl, poured the soup over it, and called it a meal. I was pretty sure my creation wouldn't make it into the recipe books, but it killed my hunger.

The springs rebelled as I crawled into bed, but I ignored them and stared at the shadow patterns on the ceiling until sleep took over. My last conscious thought was of a gorgeous blonde with bright red lips and a cocky smile.

Chapter 9

THE SUN WAS beating down, the sand was soft, and the scent of Coppertone suntan lotion was thick in the air. A warm breeze blew in off the water, and a bevy of bikinied beauties paraded by, each one more lovely than the last. Then the damned Harley roared to life, and I was back in my drab digs.

I'd forgotten to pick up coffee, and knowing the cupboard was bare, decided to hit Sonny's Donuts for coffee and a donut on my way in. Sonny Nguyen had owned and operated the place for sixteen years, ever since moving to the United States from Vietnam. I'm not sure why he landed in Rockland. As far as I know, he's the only representative from that part of the world anywhere around. But I'm glad he did. His donuts are the best in town, and the vanilla custard-filled is my favorite. I figure it's a complete breakfast since it's made with eggs, flour, and milk. Chocolate frosted is Lucille's favorite, so I got one to go. Despite our constant verbal sparring, I like her a lot.

The phone was ringing when I entered my office. I hung my trench coat and hat on the rack and answered.

"Nolan."

"Detective, this is Nora Belzer. I was talking with Benny last evening when I picked up my car. He owns Gunnerson's Garage, you know."

"Yes, I know."

"He told me that Walt, he's the one who usually works on my car, hasn't been to work for two days, and no one knows where he is."

"Uh-huh."

"Well, I saw Walt Wednesday evening."

"You did?"

"Yes. I was driving home from my friend's house when I saw him. I was stopped at a red light at Third and Harvester when a car pulled up next to me. A blond woman I hadn't seen before was driving, and Walt was sitting next to her."

"What time was that?"

"It was seven-fifteen."

"How do you know that?"

"Because I was listening to the radio, and they announced the time while I was stopped."

"What did the woman look like?"

"I couldn't see her very well. She was looking straight ahead, and her face was in shadow. I didn't see much other than her blond hair. I could see Walt good. The streetlight was shining right on his face. He looked my way, and I gave him a wave, but I guess he didn't see me 'cause he didn't wave back."

"Do you know where they went?"

"I have no idea."

"What kind of car was it?"

"I know it was a Buick because it had the four holes along the side. It looked pretty new, but I don't know what model it was."

"How about the color?"

"It was light, maybe gray or cream."

"Did you get the license plate number?"

"Heavens no. I didn't think to look for that. Why would I?"

"I just thought it might have caught your eye."

"Nope."

I thanked her, hung up, and dialed my buddy, Con Sunderson, at the motor vehicle's department.

"Sunderson."

"Connie, how ya be?"

"Hey, Vince. What's up?"

"I need another favor."

"Shoot."

"You familiar with the Buick Roadmaster?"

"A little, why?"

"It's the only model with four ventiports, right? You know, the four holes on the side."

"Yeah, it is, but I hear they're gonna put four on other models next year."

"I need you to put together a list of all the 1950 to 1954 Buick Roadmasters in the county. Can you do that?"

"Sure, but it's gonna take some time."

"It's important. Let me know as soon as you can."

"I'll put my best guy on it."

"Thanks, buddy. Hi to Ethel."

"Will do."

I hung up and picked up the bag containing the hair I had so skillfully retrieved last night. I didn't think it would match the other hairs we had, but I wanted to be thorough.

I took it down to Collins's dungeon and waited while he put it under the microscope. He checked it with the other hairs and told me it wasn't a match. I smiled as an image of Blondie flashed in my head.

"Thanks, Collins."

"Any time."

I grabbed another cup of coffee on the way back to my office and stood at the window drinking it while watching the action on the street. A newer car pulled into a parking space across the street. It was a light blue Buick Roadmaster. An older gentleman got out and went into Carver's. I figured he wasn't our dick dicer but, who knows, he may have a blond young wife or daughter. I jotted down the plate number.

The photo of the partial tire print from the second crime scene was sitting on my desk. I picked it up, put on my coat, and walked across the street. The tires on the car looked new, and none of the blocks I could see were missing a corner. I wondered when the tires had been replaced and where the old ones were.

I started back across the street when I heard, "Can I help you?" It was the old guy I saw get out of the car.

Thinking fast, I said, "I was just checking out your tires. They look new, and I was wondering what brand they are. I need new tires for my car."

That broke the ice, and he said, "They're Firestones. Only tire I trust. I got 'em at Hank's Tires over on Dairy Road. You know the place?"

"Yeah, I do."

"Ask for Hank. He really knows his tires. Tell him Leo sent ya."

"I'll do that, Leo. Thanks again."

He threw me a wave and drove off.

I got in my car and drove to Hank's. Dairy Road was one of the nicer residential streets in Rockland. It was lined with big elm trees and well-maintained ranch-style houses. Hanks was at the far end and seemed out of place.

The whine of a lug wrench greeted me when I parked. A mostly bald, overweight gentleman wearing blue coveralls was removing tires from an old pickup. He stood when he saw me approach.

"Are you, Hank?"

"That's me. What can I do ya for?"

I held out my shield and said, "I just spoke with an older gentleman named Leo. He said you recently changed the tires on his Buick Roadmaster."

"That I did. Leo's been coming here since my daddy ran the place."

"I'd like to see the tires you replaced if you still have them."

"I do. They're out back. Pickup day's tomorrow, so you just made it."

Hank pointed to four Firestones stacked against the back wall of the shop and, "That's them."

None of the treads matched the photos. I thanked Hank for his time and headed back to the station.

Someone had laid a copy of Friday's *Rockland Gazette* on my desk while I was gone. The picture on the front page was of me going through Anderson's car at the motel. The headline blared LOCAL MAN VANISHES, and the subtitle asked, IS HE A VICTIM OF THE MANHOOD MARAUDER?

I thought, Manhood Marauder. Seriously? The Gazette was in dire need of a new editor. Apparently, the lovely Miss Carlson had spilled the beans to the cub reporter in detail. I felt sorry for Mrs. Anderson. Now the whole town would wonder what Anderson was up to and what happened to him.

Three phone slips were stuck on the metal message spike on my desk, all from Rosemary Anderson, and marked urgent. I hoped she hadn't seen the paper. I picked up the phone and dialed her number.

"Hello."

"Mrs. Anderson, it's Detective Nolan."

Her grating voice raised in pitch and volume, and she said, "How dare you say those terrible things about my Mason. The nerve of you. You should be ashamed of yourself."

"Ma'am, I assure you that no one from the police department made any statement to the press about Mason. They must have gotten the information from someone at the motel. I'm truly sorry. It shouldn't have happened."

"You didn't talk to the paper?"

"Not about Mason, no."

"Well then, I apologize for shouting at you. I'm just so upset."

"I understand, ma'am. I'd be upset too."

"Do you have more information about what

happened?"

"Not at this time. But we're doing our best to find your husband."

"Please, let me know as soon as you find something."

"I'll do that."

"Thank you, Detective. Again, I'm sorry for accusing you."

"Not a problem."

I hung up and tossed the message slips into the circular file. Reporters. They can help, and they can hurt.

Petuski stuck his head in the door and asked if I wanted to join him for lunch; he was going to Carver's. I didn't, but he is my partner, so I grabbed my coat and hat and followed him out.

Chapter 10

THE HAM AND cheese I had for lunch was having its way with me. I closed the blinds, put my feet up on the desk, and leaned back in my chair to grab some shuteye when the phone rang. It brought me back from the edge of unconsciousness.

"Nolan."

"Vince, it's Tim. I wanted to give you an update on the prints from the motel."

Working my way back to the moment, I said, "Uh-huh."

"All of the prints from the car belong to either Mr. or Mrs. Anderson. I found Anderson's prints on the entry doorknob and phone. None of the prints on the bathroom doorknob, television, or nightstand were his. There's a thumbprint from the phone that doesn't match Anderson or any of the other prints."

"Thanks, Collins."

"You bet."

I wondered if any of the prints matched our perp. Maybe Anderson let the woman into his room, and she went about her business without touching anything other than Anderson and the blade she used. Or maybe she wore gloves. Hopefully, at least one of the prints would link our perp to the room. Now I just had to find her.

There was a message to call Sunderson stuck on my message spike. I called him.

"Sunderson."

"Hey, buddy, I see you called."

"Yeah, I've got the list of Roadmasters you wanted."

"Great. That was fast."

"We aim to please. There are thirty-three of 'em registered in the county. I'll have the list messengered over to you."

"Thanks. Hey, let's grab a drink after work one of these days."

"Sounds good. Tuesdays are usually best for me."

"Let's plan on Tuesday, then."

"You're on."

The list, including two carbon copies, arrived ten minutes later. I gave one copy to Racine and the other to Petuski and told them we were looking for a light-colored Roadmaster driven by a blond woman. I kept the original. We split up, each of us taking eleven of the names, and spread out over the county to see what we could dig up.

I was back at the station by four, and Petuski showed up twenty minutes later. Racine's list included the cars garaged in the rural part of the county, so she didn't make it back until after five.

Nineteen of the thirty-three vehicles were eliminated because they were dark-colored. Five of the light-colored cars we tracked down were owned and driven by dark-haired people, but we still checked the tires to see if any of them had a torn and broken tread block that matched our tire-print photo. That left nine we were unable to locate. Racine agreed to follow up on the nine later in the evening when people were more likely to be home. Petuski, the gallant knight that he is, said he'd go with her. I could tell by Lila's eye roll that she was less than thrilled with the idea but reluctantly agreed. There was safety in numbers, especially after dark.

My phone rang as I was packing up to call it a day.

"Nolan."

"Detective, Nolan?"

It was a woman's voice. "Yes."

"I read in the paper about Mason Anderson."

"Uh-huh. Who is this?"

"I'd rather keep my name out of it, but there's some stuff you should know about that man."

"What's that?"

"Well, he's a philanderer."

"How do you know that?"

"Detective, I don't want this to get back to Rosemary. She's his wife, you know."

"Yes, I know."

"Rosemary's a friend of mine, and I don't want to see her hurt. She's such a lovely woman. And a good wife. Can you promise me she won't find out?"

"No, ma'am, I can't make that promise, but I'll do what I can to protect her."

"Thank you, Detective. I understand. Oh, this is difficult. Anyway, I've seen Mason's car parked at that motel where you found it more than once over the years.

"One time, I saw him go into one of the rooms with our minister's wife. He had his arm around her, and it didn't look like they were going to a prayer meeting. I was so upset I didn't go to church for weeks. I just couldn't bear to look at her."

"When was that?"

"Oh, it's been four or five years now."

"Anything else?"

"Well, rumor had it that he and Walt Peterson raped a woman here in town when they were teenagers."

"Really? I hadn't heard that."

"There's no reason you would have. I heard she didn't report it because she was too embarrassed and scared. Her husband had left her a couple of years before, so she packed up her boy and left town. I don't believe she's been heard from since."

"And how is it you know this?"

"Well, I don't *know* it. It's just what I heard back then, maybe twenty years ago."

"Who'd you hear it from?"

"Mrs. Smith told me. Evelyn Smith. She lived across the street from the woman at the time."

"Is she still around?"

"I believe so. I haven't seen her in years. Last I heard she was living at Pleasanton Manor. She must be in her nineties now if she's still with us."

"Do you remember the name of the woman who was raped or her boy's name?"

"No. If I ever knew their names, I've forgotten. I do remember seeing the boy out playing in the yard one time when I was over visiting Evelyn. A nice-looking young man, as I recall."

"Do you know where they moved?"

"No. Evelyn may know."

"Thanks for the call. What's your name, again?"

"Good one, Detective."

She hung up.

I called Pleasanton Manor and asked if Evelyn Smith lived there.

A woman's twangy voice said, "May I ask who's calling?"

"Detective Nolan, Rockland PD."

"Are you family?"

"No, ma'am."

"Detective, Mrs. Smith passed away two years ago. I'm sorry."

"I see. Thank you."

She said, "My pleasure," then realizing that didn't sound appropriate, having just informed me of a death, said, "I, uh, don't mean pleasure. It's certainly not a pleasure. I, uh—"

I cut her off and said, "I get it," and hung up.

It was Saturday night, and the office was quiet. Racine and Petuski were out checking Roadmasters, and most of the cops who were on duty were out driving their beats. It was just Lucille, the desk sergeant, a new guy whose name I couldn't remember, and me.

I heard Jim calling me, so I unlocked the desk drawer, took him out, and poured three fingers into the glass I'd used earlier. An Old Gold found its way out of the pack, and I lit it with the silver Zippo lighter my dad gave me. He had used it from the time he started smoking at age ten until his death six years ago. It brought back memories, some good, some not so good.

I stood at the window and watched the Saturday night activity on the street.

Mary Francis was arranging two dozen red roses in a vase for a guy who stood, nervously turning his hat in his hands. I guessed it was a gift to the wife for some indiscretion she hadn't forgiven.

Carver's weekend busboy was sweeping the sidewalk in front of the place while taking a smoke break. He leaned on the broom and ogled two broads that must have been twice his age. They turned in unison and gave him the bird. He just smiled and waved. He was a cocky little shit.

It had been a long week, and I didn't feel like being in a crowd. Even the Nail would be busier than I like. It was time to head to the hovel. Maybe I'd whip up a grilled cheese sandwich, catch *The Jackie Gleason Show*, and turn in early for a change.

Chapter 11

A THUNDERCLAP RATTLED the windows and woke me at six on Sunday morning. Rivulets of rain raced down the glass, and the wind was whipping the hell out of the elm in front of my building. I was glad I'd hit the hay when I did.

Stopping at the market on my way home last night meant I didn't have to slog through the rain to get breakfast. I put on the coffee, poured a bowl of cornflakes, and cut up a banana on it.

My feet were freezing on the bare floor, so I pulled on my slippers and stood over the floor grate, eating the odd-shaped corn.

Sunday is my day off, so I didn't have to hurry down to the station. Petuski was there and could handle any calls that came in on the ding-dong disaster. At least I hoped he could. I took my cereal bowl to the kitchen, turned on the tap, waited for the brown water to clear, and rinsed it.

As usual, the paperboy had managed to get the Sunday paper about halfway to my door. I figured the old lady next door would call the cops if I ran out in my boxers, so I threw on a terry robe and made a mad dash for it. My slippers made a squishy sound as they slapped the wet sidewalk.

I kicked off my soaked slippers and stood over the heater grate to dry off and warm up. The paperboy had done a fair job of wrapping the paper, so only one corner was wet. I leaned against the wall and skimmed through the pages, looking for anything about the tallywacker tragedy. Nothing. Miss Cub Reporter apparently hadn't gotten wind of the possible rape connection yet. That was a good thing.

My favorite part of the Sunday paper is, and always has been, the funnies. I read all of them, even the ones I don't find funny. *Dick Tracy* and *Lil Abner* are my all-time favorites. *Tracy* because he's a detective like me, and *Abner* for the sassy-looking hillbilly blonde.

I usually like to spend my Sunday hiking out along the river, but the weather put the kibosh on outdoor activity. I didn't want to spend the whole day sitting in my musty apartment, staring at the bare walls, so I decided to follow up with Pleasanton Manor and see if Evelyn Smith had any close friends there that are still alive and alert.

I dialed the Manor, and the same nasal-sounding voice I'd heard yesterday picked up.

"Pleasanton Manor, Gayle speaking."

"Gayle, Detective Nolan."

"Good morning, Detective."

"I want to follow up on our conversation yesterday. Do you know if Mrs. Smith had any close friends who still live at Pleasanton?"

"Why, yes. She and Mrs. Palmer were very close. They went for walks together and always ate their meals at the same table. Cynthia, that's Mrs. Palmer, still lives here."

"Is she mentally alert?"

"Ohhh, yes. I call her the firecracker."

"Is she there today, and would it be possible to come out and talk with her?"

"She's here. I saw her walk by a minute ago. Let me put you on hold, and I'll ask her if she'll meet with you."

"Thank—"

She clicked off, and Muzak was droning mindless elevator music in my ear. I was trying to identify the nondescript tune when Gayle clicked back on.

"Are you still there, Detective?"

"I'm here."

"I just spoke with Mrs. Palmer, and she said she'd be happy to talk with you today. Anytime is good for her except from twelve to one and five to six when she eats her meals, and then again at seven-thirty when she watches *The Jack Benny Show*."

"Tell her I'll be there in an hour."

"OK, Detective. See you then."

The rain had slowed to a drizzle by the time I got out of the shower, but the wind was still doing its best to uproot trees. I slipped on my rubbers, buttoned up my trench coat, grabbed my umbrella in one hand, held my fedora on my head with the other, and sprinted to the car.

The manor was a ten-minute drive from my apartment. I told Gayle I'd be there in an hour, and I still had another twenty-five minutes before the hour was up. I didn't want to get there early because I know how the elderly depend on a strict schedule. My grandmother used to complain if guests showed up five minutes before they said they'd be there. I decided to swing by the station to see if Lila and Petuski had any luck tracking down the Roadmasters.

Petuski was at his desk, lost in the latest *Mad* comic book. I walked up and stood behind him. He let out an occasional chuckle but didn't notice me. The guy was still a kid at heart, although, I have to admit, I've glanced through the comic a couple of times, and it is pretty funny.

I tapped him on the shoulder, and he flew out of his chair, knocking files off his desk in the process.

"Morning, sunshine."

"Darn it, boss. You coulda given me a heart attack."

I laughed.

"That's not funny. You could have."

"Settle down, sweet pea. You'll live."

His heart rate slowed, and he sat back down.

"What's the word on the Roadmasters?"

"We found eight of 'em. All driven by dark-haired folks except one, and it belonged to a forty-five-year-old blond man. We checked all the tires and didn't find any with a cracked and broken tread block. Neighbors told us the one we didn't find belongs to a young couple with two kids, all dark-haired. The family left on a road trip two weeks ago and aren't expected back until sometime next week. Wrong hair color aside, they weren't around during the time in question."

"Hmm, looks like we're looking for someone from out of the county."

"What do we do now?"

"Keep our eyes and ears open. The perp could be from anywhere. We don't have the resources to check the whole country."

"I thought this was your day off. What are you doin' here?"

"Restless. I didn't want to sit around home and was curious about what you found out last night. I'm heading out to Pleasanton Manor to talk with an old gal who knew Evelyn Smith. Hopefully, she knows something about the woman who was raped."

"Want me to come along?"

"Na. I got it. It won't take long. I'll see you tomorrow."

Lucille was standing at the door to the fort holding out a box of donuts when I walked past.

"For you, my love."

"Aww, you shouldn't have."

"I know, but it's a Sunday ritual."

I said, "I like rituals," as I grabbed a jelly-filled, blew her a kiss, and left.

The first thing I heard when I entered the manor was Gayle shouting, "Cynthia," at a little old lady at the far end of the lobby. She stopped, turned to Gayle, and shouted, "What?" Gayle pointed at me at said, "It's Detective Nolan."

Cynthia Palmer scrunched up her face and studied me through a pair of thick-lensed glasses that sat catawampus on a nose too big for the face it was attached to. She wore a shapeless, floral-patterned dress, support hose that sagged around her ankles, and black orthopedic shoes.

I gave her a wave, and she hobbled toward me. Her left hip was shot, causing her to rock back-and-forth as she walked.

She threw out a hand as she approached and said, "Hi ya, cutie. I've been waitin' for ya."

She was definitely a firecracker. I saw Gayle smile and shake her head.

"Mrs. Palmer—"

"Stop right there. It's Cynthia, or we don't go any further."

"Cynthia, I'm Detective Nolan."

"I know who you are."

"Can we go somewhere and talk."

Her dry, cracked lips split a smile, and she said, "Are you trying to pick me up, young fella?"

I let out a laugh and said, "No, Ma'am. I just want to ask you some questions."

"That's too bad. Follow me."

She led me to a pair of upholstered chairs in front of the lobby fireplace. She sat, using her arms for support until the weight was too much, then fell the rest of the way into the chair.

"So, what do ya wanna know, bubby?"

I liked the old girl. She was cheeky, a quality I admire in a woman. Guess that's why I find the forensics professor so attractive, that and those legs that go all the way to the floor.

"You knew Evelyn Smith?"

"I sure did. Best friend I ever had. Why do you ask?"

"Did she ever talk to you about a woman, a neighbor of hers, that was raped about twenty years ago?"

"You must be talkin' about Mary McDaniels. Sure, she talked about her. What do you wanna know?"

"Did Evelyn know who raped her?"

"Mary told her a couple of young fellas from town did it."

"Did she know their names?"

"She told me once, but it was a long time ago. One was Matt or Martin, something like that."

"Could it have been Mason? Mason Anderson?"

"Now that you mention it, I think that was his name."

"Do you remember the other boy's name?"

"No, it's been too long. My memory ain't what it used to be."

"Isn't."

"What?"

"Nothing."

"Does the name Walt Peterson ring a bell?"

"Can't say that it does."

"Did Evelyn ever mention Mary's son?"

"Not that I recall."

"I understand Miss McDaniels moved sometime after the rape. Did Evelyn say where she moved?"

"I remember her telling me that she moved, but I don't recollect where."

"Did you ever see Miss McDaniels?"

"Nope."

"Do you know if Miss McDaniels had blond hair?"

"Heavens, no. Why would I?"

"Just checking."

I stood, extended my hand, and said, "Cynthia, you've been most helpful. Thank you."

She took my hand and held on to it.

"It's been a pleasure, Detective. Why don't you come back and see me sometime? Maybe for dinner?"

She winked and gave my hand a squeeze before releasing it.

I said, "I'll think about it," and turned to leave.

She let out a mischievous chuckle and said, "You do that, handsome."

The rain had picked up again. I hoisted my umbrella and made a mad dash for the car.

Chapter 12

THE TEMPERATURE HAD dropped another ten degrees during my visit with Cynthia. I started the car and kicked the heater to high. A white fog immediately covered the windshield. I cracked the window a smidge to circulate the air and wiped the glass in front of me with my glove. That cleared the fog but left beads of water in my field of view. I found a napkin on the floor from my last visit to Sonny's Donuts and used it to sop up most of the water beads so I could see to drive.

The wipers beat a staccato rhythm as I drove the green bomb out of the parking lot and turned toward downtown. I made a left onto Greenfield Avenue—the name given to Route 14 as it passes through town—and hit a red light at the first intersection.

I was fiddling with the radio, trying to find a country and western station, when a car pulled up next to me. The first thing I noticed when I looked over was the four distinctive ventiports of a Buick Roadmaster. That got my attention, and I stopped playing with the radio.

The rain made it hard to see, but I could tell it was a young man driving with a young woman sitting next to him. Both had dark-brown hair. Two munchkin faces were pressed against the backseat window giving me a blank stare. Both faces suddenly transformed into the scariest look a little kid can muster, their tongues shot out, and they burst into giggles before disappearing. It reminded me of when I was a kid.

The light changed, and the Buick took off. I thought about following it but changed my mind. They had dark hair, the plates were from out of state, and the gray color was too dark to have been mistaken as light by Delores Conroy and Nora Belzer.

My digs were depressing enough on a sunny day. On a rainy day like today, forget it. I had no desire to spend the afternoon standing over the heater grate, staring out the window, and drinking alone.

It was a perfect day for the Nail. It usually wasn't crowded on Sunday afternoon, and the rain would keep lots of the regulars at home. Jimmy, my favorite barkeep, would be pouring the drinks. He had thick fingers, and that's what he used to measure a pour. He was tending bar there when I first found the place and knew Jim Beam Black was my drink. One was always set up at my regular seat by the time I reached the bar. Today was no exception.

"Vince, my man, how be ya?"

"Cold and wet."

"I hear that. The place has been dead. But after the craziness of last night, it's fine with me."

Jimmy went back to washing glasses, and I lit a smoke. There wasn't a dame in the joint, just the die-hard regulars that hell freezing over wouldn't keep away.

Webb Pierce's number one country and western single, "Slowly," was flowing from the jukebox like sweet syrup, the steel guitar singing right along with him. Jake Dudeker was standing next to the dartboard, twirling a dart in his hand, and staring at me with a cocky grin on his face. He was the Nail's self-proclaimed darts guru and the only guy who could consistently whip my butt. He held up the dart and waved me over.

I was still smarting from our last encounter when he skunked me three consecutive legs, winning the set. I know I can beat that clown, but he always seems to bring the challenge after I've had too many conversations with my friend Mr. Beam.

Today would be different. I picked up my glass and walked to the board.

"Detective."

I nodded. "Jake."

"Ready to get your clock cleaned?"

I wanted to knock the smirk off his face, but instead said, "Dream on, sucker."

Jake tipped his head toward the board, signaling me to take my nine warm-up throws. I did, and Jake took his.

"Go ahead, Vince, you throw first to see who starts."

I did and hit a bullseye.

"Very impressive, my friend."

We weren't just friends, we were combatants, and Jake knew it. He threw and hit the green ring just outside of the bullseye.

"Well, Detective, it looks like it's your day. Wanna play 501?"

"Sure. But only one set. I don't want to spend

my day humiliating you."

"My, but we're cocky today."

I gave a chuckle and threw. Another bullseye. I won three legs in a row and skunked *him* this time.

Jake extended his hand and said, "Well played, my friend. Let me buy you a drink."

He followed me back to my spot at the bar, and we ordered. Jimmy set the drinks down, and Jake raised his glass in a toast.

"Here's to kicking your ass next time."

"Good luck with that."

We did the obligatory glass clink, and I said, "You've lived here all your life. Did you ever know Mary McDaniels?"

"Know her? I dated her for a couple of months. Nice lady."

"And you know she was raped?"

"Yeah, I heard that. Terrible. Just terrible. It happened about a year after we stopped going out. She moved away not too long after."

"Did she ever tell you who raped her?"

"No. I didn't see her again after we stopped dating. There was a rumor going around that it was a couple of local boys from the high school. But nothing ever came of it that I know of."

"Do you know where she moved?"

"Not specifically, but I heard it was some-where in the South."

"Did you know her boy?"

"David? Sure. He was a great kid. Loved his momma. I always thought he was kind of a momma's boy. But a real good kid."

"How old was the kid?"

"He was seven when I dated Mary."

"Do you know where he is?"

"No. He left with his mom, and I haven't seen him since."

"What color was Mary's hair?"

"Blonde. She was the real deal. No bleach blonde for her. Hey, what's with all the questions about Mary and David? She in trouble?"

"Not that I know of. Just checking."

"Yeah, right."

Jake finished his drink, promised to kick my butt next time, and left.

I watched him walk out and wondered if Mary McDaniels was our salami slicer. Assuming the rape rumor is true—and I believe it is because so many people say they heard it—she definitely had motive and blond hair to boot. I had to find her.

Besides Jimmy, sawdust on the floor, and darts, one of my favorite things about the Nail is the pickled eggs. The first owner of the bar was a German immigrant named Müller. He brought the tradition over, and it's been a Nail staple ever since. Lots of people don't like them, but I think the tangy flavor is the perfect compliment to alcohol of any kind. I pointed to the jar that always sat behind the bar, and Jimmy brought it over. I used the tongs to extract one of the delicacies.

"Thanks, Jimmy. Hey, will you put in an order for a burger, well done, and some fries? I need something to absorb the booze."

"You got it, boss."

I held up my glass and said, "Oh, and a refill."

"Comin' up."

I was savoring my first bite of the zesty egg when I felt a hand on my shoulder, and a sultry voice said, "Want some company, sailor?"

I stopped chewing, looked up, and was surprised to see the blonde.

"Professor."

"Please, Christine. I haven't even started classes yet."

I stared at her, not quite knowing what to say.

She pointed to the empty stool next to me and said, "Mind if I join you?"

"Be my guest."

She removed her rain scarf and coat, set them on the bar, and sat down.

"I'm surprised to see you in a joint like this."

"Why's that?"

"You seem like a classy dame."

"I am, but I still enjoy sawdust on the floor and some country and western now and again. Besides, I saw your ride out front and thought you might like some company on this dreary day."

"What are you drinking? It's on me for the ride the other night."

"Thank you, sir. A martini, dirty, three olives dirty, heavy on the gin, light on the vermouth."

"You got it."

I motioned Jimmy over, introduced him to Christine, and gave him her order.

Christine looked at what was left of my egg and said, "What in the world are you eating?"

"Pickled egg. Ever had one?"

"No."

I got Jimmy's attention and had him bring the pickle jar. Christine looked skeptical but reached in with the tongs and grabbed one.

She took a bite and said, "Oh my God, these are amazing. I've never heard of them before."

"They're big in German bars, especially with beer. The original owner of the Nail was from Germany."

Jimmy brought Christine's drink along with my burger.

I pointed to the burger and said, "You hungry? Burgers are great here."

"No, thanks, I had a late breakfast."

She finished her egg, sipped the martini, and said, "Mmm, good martini."

"Yeah, Jimmy's the best."

She wiped the corners of her mouth with a napkin and said, "Anything shakin' on the dismemberment case?"

"We're following up on all leads, but so far, nothing to write home about."

"Any connection to the two missing men?"

I gave her a look and said, "You know I can't talk about an ongoing investigation."

"I know it's an open case, and I'm not with the department, but forensics is my field, and I'm willing to help if I can, no charge."

It was a tempting offer. I was the only one with experience working the case. Petuski's a nice guy, but he's green, with little practical experience. I could use a second opinion.

"Whatever I say stays between us, capisce?"

"Of course. Don't forget. I was with NYPD for

fifteen years. This is not my first rodeo."

"About the missing men. Rumor has it they raped a woman here in town twenty years ago when they were still in high school. Apparently, she never reported it, so the police weren't involved."

"Is she still in town?"

"I was told she moved shortly after the rape, somewhere in the South. Don't know where yet."

"I'd track her down ASAP. Penile amputation is typically a woman-on-man revenge crime. She'd definitely have a motive."

"That she would. Hopefully, we can find someone who knows where she went."

She pointed to my fries and said, "May I?"

"Help yourself. I'm done."

I finished my drink while Blondie helped herself to my fries. The rain was still coming down in waves that whipped past the window and on down the street. The professor picked up her drink, saw it was empty, and set it back down.

I didn't want her to leave and said, "It's my day off. I'm having another. You?"

"Sure. Why not?"

I got Jimmy's attention, pointed to our drinks, and held up two fingers.

It was a nice way to spend a rainy Sunday. Hell, any Sunday. I hadn't spent time with a dame outside of work since my ex, Karen; that was over a year ago. And the last few years with her was no picnic.

Blondie was smart, candy for the eyes, and way too young for me. But I wasn't about to let that get in the way of my day off.

We finished our drinks, and I challenged her to a game of pool. She accepted. I won the coin toss and broke. It was my only win. She ran the table, then gave me the cocky smile I remembered from the other night, and said, "Had enough, sailor?"

I looked at her, shook my head, and said, "Who are you, lady?"

"Christine Martin, top-ranked NYPD billiards player four years running."

I said, "God, help me," paid Jimmy for the drinks, and we left.

The billiards queen occupied my thoughts on the drive home. It was the best afternoon I'd had in a long time.

Chapter 13

MONDAY MORNING WAS the flip side of Sunday. The sun was shining, birds were flitting from tree to tree singing, and it was at least twenty degrees warmer. October, go figure.

The blonde danced around in my head while I whipped up pancakes and bacon. It was the most cooking I'd done in weeks. Must be the result of spending quality time with a quality dame; something else I hadn't done in a long time.

I showered, then ironed a fresh shirt and steamed the wrinkles out of my well-worn suit, all in anticipation of running into the blonde again. I was amazed at the influence a skirt could have on a guy, even one like me.

My phone was ringing when I stepped into the office. I tossed my fedora on the rack and answered.

"Nolan."

"Good morning, Detective. This is Clarice Weldon from the Starlight Motel. Emma Carlson told me to call."

"Yes, Miss Weldon, what can I do for you?"

"Well, Detective, I'm the maid for the motel. I clean the rooms, do the laundry, that sort of thing."

"Uh-huh."

"Well, I was off the day you was there."

"Were."

"What?"

"Nothing. Go on."

"Emma told me what you found, so I thought I'd better tell you what I seen."

I jerked the phone away from my ear to avoid any further dialectical damage. I wanted to reach through the phone and wring her scrawny neck. Instead, I put the phone back to my ear and said, "What did you see?"

"I stayed late last Tuesday to catch up on laundry. I happened to look out the door when a blond lady and a man come out of room twelve. She was tall, maybe five foot ten or eleven. He seemed like something was wrong with him."

"What do you mean?"

"Well, he was walking slow, taking baby steps with his feet spread apart. He had his hands behind his back. I didn't hear nothing, but it sure looked like he was hurting."

"Can you describe the blonde?"

"No. They was too far away."

"Did you see where they went?"

"They went to her car, at least I think it was her car. She helped the man get in, and when he turned, it looked like his hands was tied behind his back. The lady got in and drove off."

"What kind of car was it?"

"I have no idea. I don't know one car from the other. It was shiny. Looked new to me. Oh, and it had those four holes on the side."

"Was it a dark or light color?"

"Light. But I don't know what color. It was too far away, and it was dark out."

"Do you know which way they went?"

"No. I couldn't see the road from where I was."

"Thank you for calling, Miss Weldon. I appreciate your help. Let me know if you think of anything else about what you saw."

"I will, Detective."

The call disconnected.

Anderson apparently left the motel alive, hurting, but alive. I wondered if a man could survive after parting ways with his John Thomas. I picked up the phone and called Doc Williams.

"This is Doctor Williams."

"Doc, it's Vince."

"Vince, how are you? How's the investigation going?"

"I'm fine, thanks. The case is moving slow, but we're making progress."

"Good to hear."

"I've got a question for you. Can a guy survive after having his dick cut off?"

"Oh, sure. It's hard to bleed to death from the loss of a small member like the penis or a finger. Even loss of a large member such as an arm or leg can be survivable. The body is good at protecting itself from blood loss. Arteries will spasm and clamp off blood flow. And the loss of blood causes the body to divert blood flow away from extremities and toward vital organs, slowing bleeding and allowing blood to clot."

"So our dorkless dandies may still be alive?"

"Yes, although your parlance is somewhat questionable, they may still be alive as long as they weren't subjected to further harm."

"Hey, Doc, Walt Peterson wasn't a patient of yours by any chance, was he?"

"I saw him once about a year ago. Why."

"What did you see him for?"

"Vince, you know I can't breach patient confidentiality. You're asking me to go beyond my duties as coroner."

"I know, but Walt is missing, and we've got a disco stick with type B negative blood on it. Come on, Doc, I just need to know his blood type if you have it. You know I can get a subpoena?"

"Yeah, yeah, I know. Look, I didn't tell you this, agreed?"

"Agreed."

"Give me a minute."

He set the phone down, and I heard a file drawer open, followed by paper shuffling. He got back on the line and said, "B negative."

"Thanks, Doc. You're a great help."

A click told me he'd hung up.

I felt a bit squeamish after our conversation and pulled out my friend Jim. Mr. Beam always seemed to set the nerves straight.

An Old Gold found its way out of the pack. I lit it with my dad's old Zippo and stood at the window, engaging in one of my favorite pastimes, watching Mary Francis.

Unfortunately, she wasn't about. But it got me thinking that without my manhood, this exercise would be pointless.

The department liaison officer provided the *Gazette* with photos of Anderson and Peterson on Saturday, along with a request to contact

Rockland PD with any information concerning their whereabouts. After talking with Doc, I was hopeful we might find those guys alive. At least I thought I was hopeful, but I couldn't wrap my mind around going through life without the trouser snake. I wondered if a guy would still get horny. I guessed he would as long as the bag of nuts was still attached.

My message spike had two messages stuck on it. The first was from Lydia Kroger, marked urgent. I picked up the phone and dialed.

The receiver was picked up, but no one said anything. I could hear rustling sounds like papers being shuffled, but no voice. After a moment, I said, "Hello?"

Nothing but rustling sounds.

Finally, I heard a throat being cleared, and an ancient voice said, "Hello?"

"Lydia Kroger?"

"Yes."

"This is Detective Nolan from Rockland PD. You left a message to call you."

"Oh?"

"Yes. I have a message that you called."

"Who is this?"

"Detective Nolan from the Rockland Police Department."

"Oh, the police. Yes, I called."

More paper shuffling.

"Just a minute, let me put my newspaper down."

"Take your time."

"There. Now, who is this again?"

"Detective Nolan."

"Detective, I saw the picture of those boys that are lost, and I think I know where they are."

"Really? Where are they?"

"Well, I live next to the old Bartley place. I was good friends with them. They were the best neighbors, but both Emma and John passed years ago. Nobody's lived there since."

"Uh-huh."

"The place is always quiet as a tomb. You can imagine with nobody there. But the last couple of days, I've been hearing strange sounds coming from it."

"What kind of sounds?"

"Just like somebody movin' around. A few times, I heard voices and a loud noise like something dropped."

"And you just started hearing the noises?"

"Yes. My daughter has been insisting for years that I get a hearing aid, and I finally gave in and got one."

"So you started hearing the noises after you got the hearing aid?"

"That's right. There may have been noise before that I didn't hear. But I hear them now. I thought you should know."

"Have you seen anyone at the house?"

"No, not in years. And I don't see any lights. The electricity's been off ever since Emma passed."

I thanked her, got the address for the Bartley house, and hung up.

The second message was from a Madam Adelle. Madam Adelle? I wondered if she was a real madam and calling because one of her johns was giving her trouble. I wasn't aware of any cat houses in the area, but you never know.

I dialed, and a sultry voice answered.

"Hallo."

"Madam Adelle?"

"Jes."

"Detective Nolan, Rockland PD. You called?"

"Jes. I know where the mans are that you're looking for."

"Really? Where are they?"

"At the bottom of a lake two miles north of town. They are dead. I'm sorry."

"How do you know that?"

"Do you know tarot cards?"

"I've heard of them. Don't know anything about it."

"I've been reading cards for thirty years. I want to help you find these mans, so I asked the cards, where are these mans? You look there. You will find."

The line went dead.

"Hello?"

Nothing. She hung up on me. Nothing like a good missing person mystery to bring the kooks out. I knew for a fact that there weren't any lakes north of town.

There was a knock at my door, followed by a bright-eyed Petuski.

"Morning, boss."

"Norb."

"How was your day off?"

"Good. Listen, I just talked with an old gal who said she's been hearing noises coming from the abandoned house next to her. Thinks it might have something to do with the missing men. It's probably nothing, but let's head over there and check it out."

On the way over, I asked Norb how it was going with Lila. He looked out the side window and said they hadn't seen much of one another lately because she wanted to take it slow. I imagined that not seeing much of one another meant not at all, except at work, and taking it slow to Lila meant coming to a complete stop and letting Petuski down gently. I felt sorry for the guy. He's a good man, just immature, and not very adept with the ladies.

I stopped the car in front of the address Lydia gave me. To call it abandoned was an understatement. The address was only visible from the stain left on the siding where numbers were once attached, the first step to the porch was broken, a couple of windows were missing glass where kids had probably dared one another to break them, and bushes and trees covered the once-attractive cottage.

I looked at Petuski and said, "Think anybody's home?"

"Ya, probably."

"Let's check it out."

The front door was locked. We split up. Petuski went left, I went right, and we met at the back of the house. A dog ran over from the neighbor's yard with its tail wagging, smelled the seat of Norb's pants, and ran back. Made me glad I'm not a dog. There are better ways to get to know someone.

The back door was open a crack, so I gave it a

push, and we went in. The kitchen floor tiles were yellowed and buckled, water stains marbled the ceiling, a rusted fridge leaned against one wall, its door was open, and an old box of baking soda that had long ago absorbed its last odor spilled its contents on the top self.

The place smelled of urine. A ragged couch was pushed against the living room wall, and an orange crate served as a coffee table. Beer cans and whiskey bottles littered the floor, and a tin can on top of the crate was stuffed with cigarette butts. It was a place where local teens and winos had been doing their thing long before the old lady got her hearing aid.

The house was empty, and there was no evidence the meat stick marauder's victims had been there.

I noticed a used condom stuck to the bottom of Petuski's shoe as we walked out the back door. I didn't say anything, hoping to get his reaction when he noticed it. He didn't, and it had fallen off by the time we reached the car.

Chapter 14

I DROPPED PETUSKI off at the station. He was going to canvas the neighborhood around where Mary McDaniel's had lived to see if anyone knew where she'd moved.

Tom Kingsley was the principal at Grant Elementary School and had been for twenty-five years. It was the school David McDaniels would have attended before he moved. I've known Tom ever since moving to Rockland. He bowled on a team that Con, Ethel, Karen, and I consistently beat. I wanted to see if he knew where David and his mom had moved.

Grant was a dreary looking building with GRANT ELEMENTARY SCHOOL memorialized in concrete near the top of the front wall. A flagpole stood in the center of the lawn, and a stiff breeze was giving Old Glory a workout. One of the teachers had her class in two lines on the playground, facing one another in a fierce game of Red Rover. A skinny-legged girl was racing toward the opposite line, arms pumping, and dress flapping as the two boys she was headed toward held each others' hands in a death grip.

Tom was in his office looking very official in his white shirt, tan slacks, navy blazer, and hush puppies. He saw me walking down the hall and gave me a wave.

"Vince, it's been a while."

"It has. How're you doing? Still a crappy bowler?"

"I guess. Haven't played in years. You humiliated me too many times."

"Sorry about that."

"No you're not."

"You're right."

"So what brings you to the halls of higher learning?"

"Do you remember David McDaniels? He'd have been here twenty years ago."

"Name sounds familiar."

"There was a rumor that his mom had been raped by a couple of local boys, and she moved not too long after."

"Oh, sure. I remember that, and I remember David now. He was in third grade when he left; a good kid, smart, got along with everybody. The last couple of months he was here, he was a changed kid."

"How's that?"

"Didn't talk, didn't smile, didn't do his homework, and he got in a fight with one of the boys from his class. Very unlike David. It made me wonder if the rape rumor was true."

"Do you know where they moved?"

"No but let me check in the archives. We keep a file on all students that attend Grant. It's been a long time, but we should still have it."

"I appreciate it, Tom. Thanks."

"No problem. Wait here, and I'll run down to the basement and check."

A bell went off, signaling the end of recess. It was loud and jarring and made me jump. A few seconds later, the hall reverberated with the sound of laughing, shouting kids, and the clatter of running feet. A teacher tried in vain to slow the stampede and kept repeating, "Slow down, children. Walk."

The air in Tom's office smelled of dust and chalk, with a hint of coffee that had been brewed earlier in the day. The odor of sweaty sneakers wafted through the office as the kids flew by. I couldn't imagine spending my days looking after a bunch of ankle-biters.

Tom returned carrying a thin manila folder. His hush puppies squeaked with each step on the freshly waxed floor.

He said, "Found it," as he sat behind his well-worn, wooden desk. I could see the name McDANIELS, DAVID neatly typed at the top of the folder. Tom opened it and shuffled through a few papers.

"Ah, here it is. David left us in April 1934. Looks like we transferred his records to Pittman Elementary School in Saxton, South Carolina. That's the last record we have for him."

"Do you have an address and phone number?"

"No phone number, but the address we have is 746 West Ninth Street."

I stood, extended my hand, and said, "Thanks, Tom. I appreciate your help."

"Anytime, my friend."

"Let me know if you ever want me to shame you again at the lanes."

He extended his middle finger, then quickly retracted it when he remembered where he was.

"Get outta here."

I picked up a sandwich on my way back to the office and was sitting at my desk eating it when Petuski walked in.

"Oh, sorry, boss. Didn't know you were eating. I can come back."

My mouth was full, so I shook my head and pointed at a chair. Petuski sat.

I finished chewing and said, "No problem. What'd you find out?"

"I covered all the houses within a block in every direction from where McDaniels lived. Not everyone was home, but I did talk to all the homeowners immediately surrounding her house. A couple of them were there when McDaniels lived there. Nobody had any idea where she went. Apparently, she just left one day."

"Anyone know anything about David?"

"No. Same story with him. He was just not there one day."

"Anything else?"

"No one I talked to knew anything about a rape. They said she was a loner, didn't socialize much."

"Did anyone know what kind of work she did or where she worked?"

"The old guy across the street remembered seeing her in what he thought was a waitress uniform. But he didn't know where she worked and never saw her at any of the places where he ate."

I finished my sandwich while I filled Petuski in on what I'd learned from Tom Kingsley.

"Norb, why don't you contact the county recorder, county clerk, and registrar of voters. See if any of them have anything on Mary McDaniels. Maybe she moved back here. And check the court records; there might be something in her divorce file that'll give us a clue as to where she went. I'll follow up on the waitress angle and see if I can track down her old employer."

Petuski went back to his desk, and I pulled out the yellow pages to search for restaurants. Rockland is a small town, so there weren't many listings. I started with the ones I knew had been around a long time. My fourth call was to Aunt Martha's Kitchen. Karen and I had eaten there a few times when we still liked one another, and I remembered the menu boasting it had been in business since 1925. Martha was a classy broad in her mid-fifties, and based on what I remembered about her, she must have been a real looker in her day. The line was picked up on the fifth ring.

"Aunt Martha's."

"Is this Martha?"

"Speaking."

"Martha, it's Vince Nolan with Rockland PD."

"Hey, Vince, I remember you. Haven't seen you in a while. What happened to ya?"

"I used to come in with my wife—

"I remember that."

—But since we split up, I've avoided coming in. Didn't want to stir up old memories."

"I hear that. I try to avoid thinking about my ex too."

"Listen, Martha. I'm trying to locate a gal who may have been a waitress in town about twenty years ago."

"That's a while ago."

"Yeah, it is. Did Mary McDaniels ever work for you?"

"She did. I remember her because she was a great waitress, short on personality, but an awesome waitress. Probably the best I've had. But she changed the last couple of months she was here."

"How so?"

"It was like she was in a different world: didn't make eye contact, never smiled, dropped things, and even missed work once without calling in. Then, one day she just disappeared. Didn't give notice or call in sick. Just vanished. I still have her last paycheck stuck in a drawer here someplace."

"Did she ever talk about moving?"

"Not to me."

"Did she tell you she'd been raped?"

"Oh, my God, heavens no, that's terrible. Is that true?"

"I don't know for sure, but I've heard the rumor."

"Oh, that poor woman. That would explain it."

"Do you know if she'd ever done any work besides waitressing?"

"Not that I know of. She was a stay-at-home-mom for a while, but I never heard her mention doing any other kind of work. I recall her telling me she got pregnant when she was seventeen and dropped out of the eleventh grade to have the baby. So, it's likely the only work she knew."

"Thanks, Martha. You've been a great help. Give me a call if you think of anything else that might help me find Mary."

"Will do. Hey, Vince."

"Yeah."

"Don't be a stranger. The cop discount is still good here."

"You're a doll, Martha. Thanks."

Chapter 15

THERE WAS A knock on my door, followed by Petuski's protruding ears and buck teeth.

"Boss, I checked with the recorder, county clerk, registrar of voters, and court clerk. None of 'em have anything on Mary McDaniels. Doesn't look like she ever owned property here, and marriage and divorce records would have been purged after ten years."

"Thanks, Norb."

"Anything on the waitress angle?"

"Yeah, she was a waitress at Aunt Martha's Kitchen twenty years ago, but Martha says she left without notice, and she has no idea where she went."

"What's next?"

"I'm gonna make some calls to Saxton, South Carolina, and see what I can find."

Petuski left, and I dialed the operator.

"Operator. How may I direct your call?"

"Yes, Operator, I'd like the number for Pittman Elementary School in Saxton, South Carolina."

"One moment, please."

I lit a smoke as I listened to operator chatter connecting calls all over the country. We'd come a long way since Alex Bell made the first call to his assistant, Tom Watson. The operator came back on after a couple of drags on my Old Gold.

"Sir?"

"I'm here."

"We don't show a number for Pittman Elementary School in Saxton, South Carolina."

"How about for the superintendent of schools or a high school?"

"Let me check."

More chatter. I took a couple more drags on my cig.

"Sir, I do have a number for the Saxton School District offices. Would you like me to connect you now?"

"Please."

"One moment."

There was more chatter as the call was bounced from one area to another. Then I heard a phone ringing, and a female voice answered.

"Saxton School District. How may I help you?"

"Yes, ma'am. This is Detective Nolan from the Rockland PD. I'm trying to get in touch with Pittman Elementary School."

"Oh, dear, Pittman was destroyed years ago. There was a fire, and it was a total loss."

"I'm trying to locate the mother of a boy who I understand attended Pittman about twenty years ago."

"We don't have any records from Pittman as they were all burned in the fire. What is the boy's name?"

"David. David McDaniels. And his mom is Mary McDaniels."

"Those names aren't familiar to me. Hold for a moment, and I'll check around the office to see if anyone knows them."

"Thank you."

The line went dead, and there wasn't any elevator music. It appeared Saxton was a real sleepy little town.

"Thank you for holding. I checked with everyone here, and no one has heard of them."

"Does the district keep student records from the junior and senior high schools?"

"Those are kept at the schools. Would you like those numbers?"

"Yes, please."

She gave me the numbers, and I called both schools. Neither of them had a record for David McDaniels, and no one in either office had heard of David or his mom.

I called the number for the Saxton PD, hoping someone there may know Mary's whereabouts.

"Chief Davis."

"Chief, it's Detective Vince Nolan from the Rockland PD."

"Yes, Detective, how may I help you?"

"Chief, I'm trying to locate a Mary McDaniels. It's my understanding she moved to Saxton with her son David about twenty years ago. Any chance you've heard of her?"

"Yes, as a matter of fact. Mary lived a couple of doors down from me."

"Is she still there?"

"No. Unfortunately, Mary died in an automobile accident shortly after moving here. I only met her once when I knocked on her door to introduce myself and welcome her to town. Seemed like a nice lady."

"Do you know what happened to her son, David?"

"Myla Hendricks lived next door to Mary, and she took David in until relatives could be notified."

"Did someone get David?"

"As I recall, they did, but I don't know who took him or where."

"Is Myla still in town?"

"No. She was getting up in years and passed nine or ten years ago."

"Do you know if Mary had a job?"

"She mentioned looking for a waitress job but said she hadn't had any luck when I talked to her. She was only here a week or two before the accident."

I thanked Chief Davis and asked him to contact me if he thought of anyone who may know how to locate David McDaniels. It was certain Mary was not our dork defiler. But I wanted to know if David knew anything about the rape since there is no statute of limitations for felony rape.

Telling myself I needed to cut down on the cancer sticks, I lit another one and stood at the window, wondering who had mutilated the men and why, when the phone rang.

"Nolan."

"Detective, it's Danny Sullivan."

"Uh-huh."

"I heard about Walt Peterson going missing, and I think I just saw him about fifteen minutes ago."

"What makes you think it was Peterson?"

"Walt has worked on my car before, so I know what he looks like. I'm not positive it was him, but it sure looked to be."

"Where'd you see him?"

"I was driving back from my uncle's farm a few miles north of town when I saw him walking in the woods about a hundred yards off the road."

"That's pretty far away. Did you get a look at his face?"

"Only from the side. He was tall, skinny, and walked kinda humped over, like Walt. And he was wearing a cap like Walt. I stopped the car, rolled down the window, and yelled to him, but he turned away and started walking faster."

"Do you remember where you stopped?"

"It was on the road to Waterton, about a half-mile north of Route Six. Approximately three miles north of town. You can't miss it. There's a rusted gate blocking off an overgrown grass lane leading off into the woods. He was walking down the lane. I don't know where it goes."

"What was he wearing besides the cap?"

"Blue jeans and a black jacket."

"Thanks, Mr. Sullivan. We'll check it out."

Chapter 16

NEXT TO CIGARETTES and booze, Snickers bars are my favorite poison. I check for them in every vending machine I pass. As luck would have it, or maybe bad luck, depending on your point of view, the office machine was always stocked.

I'd buzzed Petuski, filled him in on what Sullivan said, and told him to be ready to roll in five. He was wrapping up a call, so I stopped by the break room, dropped a nickel in the Vend-A-Lot, pulled the lever, and watched my prize drop. The sound of it hitting the tray always makes my mouth water, a personal fact I've not shared with anyone.

I was savoring the first bite when Norb walked up.

"Ready?"

"Just titillating the salivaries."

"What?"

"Eating a Snickers."

"Boss, you gotta watch that stuff. You're gonna get fat."

"Petuski, you need a vice."

I fired up the Ford, pulled out of the lot, and steered toward the road to Waterton. Petuski was, unfortunately, in a talkative mood and prattled on about childhood events he found amusing.

To me, they were mundane ramblings that

weren't the least bit funny. I let my mind wander to other things, like Blondie, Snickers, and the Old Golds in my pocket, occasionally showing my interest with an "Uh-huh."

We were a couple miles north of town when I saw a shimmer through the trees on the right and pulled to the shoulder.

"What are you doing?"

I ignored Petuski and got out of the car. There was a field on the other side of the trees, and in the middle of the field was a little body of water, maybe half an acre. Some farmer had dammed up a small creek, probably hoping to stock it with fish for Sunday afternoon recreation.

My mind replayed the call from the tarot-card-madam. She'd said Peterson and Anderson were in a lake two miles north of town, and we were two miles north of town, and there was a lake, small, but a lake. I lit a smoke, surveyed the area, then shook my head and mumbled, "Nah." I got back in the car.

"What was that about, Boss?"

"Nothing. Just thinking about Madam Adelle's tarot card silliness, suggesting Peterson and Anderson are at the bottom of a lake around here."

"Maybe they are. Don't you believe in the supernatural?"

"Not really, no."

"I do. Once I had my palm read, and she told me my girlfriend would break up with me. I didn't believe her because me and Mary Jane had been together for six months. We were in love. But wouldn't you know it, a week later she gave me back my ring. Made me a believer."

I looked at Petuski and thought, of course she broke up with you; you're a grammatically challenged geek, a nice guy, but a geek, nonetheless.

I checked the odometer when we crossed Route 6, so I'd know when we'd gone a half-mile. We kept our eyes on the woods to the right and found the rusted gate right where Sullivan said it would be.

A stiff breeze swinging down from the Arctic forced me to put on my trench coat. Petuski forgot his, so he turned up his sport coat collar to compensate for his forgetfulness.

The trees were thick on both sides of the road. I did a 360 but didn't see anyone. The gate was locked, so I climbed over. Norb followed.

Tall grass covered most of the lane, and saplings were doing their best to make a comeback. There was a trail of bent grass down the center where someone had recently walked. Norb and I both flinched when a covey of quail burst out of the grass fifteen feet in front of us and winged down the lane.

Five minutes into the search, I saw a small clearing on the left and what looked like the shoulder of a black jacket leaning against a tree. I held up my hand to stop Norb and pointed in the direction of the jacket.

I called out, "Walt? Walt Peterson?"

The jacket shot up, and a man started running into the woods. It happened fast, and I couldn't tell who it was through all the trees.

I shouted, "Walt, it's Vince Nolan. I just want to talk with you."

The man kept going, so Norb and I gave chase. We rounded a pile of dead brush and stopped.

Rolf Garretson was bent over, hands on his knees, and wheezing like a spent racehorse. Rolf was from somewhere in the Midwest. He'd fought in the Second World War, was one of the first on the beach at Normandy, and had seen his friends mowed down like grass. It proved too much for him to process, and, like so many others, he returned to the States a broken man. Rolf was harmless. He lived in a shack at the edge of Rockland and eked out a living mowing lawns and shoveling snow.

I caught my breath and said, "Rolf, I'm sorry. We didn't mean to scare you. Someone thought they saw Walt Peterson out here, and we were just trying to find him."

He looked into the trees, nodded, but didn't say anything.

I said, "What are you doing out here? It's cold."

It took him a while to find his words, but he finally said, "I come out sometimes to clear my head."

"I get it. It's peaceful here."

Rolf nodded.

"Can we give you a lift back to town?"

"No. I like to walk. Thanks."

"OK then. You take it easy, hear? Sorry again if we scared you."

Petuski and I walked in silence back to the car.

I pulled to the shoulder when we reached the

small lake and sat looking at it. I didn't believe in the tarot card crap, but my cop instinct was telling me we had to check it.

It was getting dark when I got back to the office and too late to search the lake. The message spike was empty, so Mr. Beam found his way out of the locked drawer. I poured a hefty shot and lit an Old Gold. The whiskey convinced me that I'd had enough for one day, and it was Nail time.

Blondie had been popping in and out of my mind all day. I didn't want to drink alone, and I wanted to see her again. I dialed her number and was surprised when she agreed to meet me. As the last of the whiskey warmed its way to my gut, I grabbed my coat and headed out.

Chapter 17

I FOUND MYSELF whistling on the drive to work Tuesday morning. Something I hadn't done in years. Having drinks with Blondie at the Nail had been a nice break from the dong disaster and a great way to end a Monday. She's a hip chick with a sarcastic sense of humor and a posterior that makes me glad I'm a man. I could dig hanging out with her as a regular thing. We'll see.

When I walked past the control room on my way to my office, Lucille was nose down in the morning paper. I said, "Good morning, sweetheart."

"Bite me."

"Love you too."

I hung up my coat and walked to the window to see if Mary Francis might kick start my morning. She wasn't in sight.

There weren't any messages on the spike, so I called Buzzy Dixson, the certified diver who does our underwater searches.

"Dixson Dives."

"Buzzy. Vince Nolan."

"Hey, man, long time no talk. What's up?"

"I need you to do a dive for me."

"Sure."

"You heard about the two guys who are missing?"

"Yeah, Peterson and Anderson. I know both

those guys."

"Well, this is a real long shot. But I got a tip that they might be in a lake north of town. I didn't know of any lake north of here, but it turns out there's a small lake, maybe half an acre, about two miles from town."

"On Dave Epperson's place. I know it. Fished it before. Some nice bass in there."

"You say his name is Epperson?"

"Yeah. It's Dave Epperson. Nice guy."

"I'll call him and get permission to check it. What's your schedule like?"

"I'm good to go anytime. Just let me know."

"Thanks, Buzzy. I'll get back to you after I talk with Epperson."

I hung up, found Epperson's number in the book, and gave him a call. He gave the OK to come out anytime, and I told him we'd be there within the hour.

Buzzy had his dive gear loaded and was ready to roll by the time I called to tell him we had the go-ahead. We agreed to meet at the entrance to the farm in half an hour.

Norb stayed at the office working other cases since I didn't hold out much hope of finding our boys at the bottom of the pond. Epperson said he hadn't seen or heard anything unusual going on at the lake, but because the house is quite a distance away, he couldn't be sure. Part of me couldn't believe I was undertaking a search based on the mental hallucinations of a mystical soothsayer.

I fired up the green bomb and headed north on Nye Avenue. Just past Nineteenth Street, a light-colored car whizzed past, going the opposite direction. I caught a glimpse of a ventiport out of my peripheral vision. There wasn't any other traffic on the street, so I flipped a U-ey and pulled up next to it at the next stoplight.

It was a light-gray 1952 Buick Special with only three ventiports. Not the car I was looking for. I looked at the driver and was met with a stare from a gray-haired prune-of-a-woman that could have frozen Satan. The light changed, and granny sped off. I drove around the block and continued to the farm.

Epperson was waiting at the end of the drive when I drove up. He looked like a Norman Rockwell painting that walked off the cover of the *Saturday Evening Post*: craggy, sunburned face; copper-colored arms; straw hat with tears in the brim; blue work shirt open at the collar with the sleeves rolled mid-bicep; Big Smith bib overalls with one strap undone, and a red rag hanging from the pocket.

Buzzy pulled in behind me. I got out as the farmer strode toward me, hand extended.

"You must be Detective Nolan."

"Guilty."

We shook hands, and I introduced him to Buzzy.

"So, you think there're bodies in my lake?"

"I don't know, but we need to check."

"Sure. Sure. Of course. Follow me then, and I'll take you down."

Buzzy and I followed him up the drive toward the house. He stopped next to a large, red barn, opened the gate, and told us to take the path to the lake. He closed the gate behind us and trailed along, not wanting to miss the action.

Epperson produced a thermos of coffee and three cups. We chewed the fat and drank the bitter brew while Buzzy suited up. It was a chilly morning, and the coffee was much appreciated.

The lake was about ten feet deep, and the water was murky. Buzzy followed a grid and worked his way back and forth from one side to the other. It was slow going since he could only see about a foot ahead.

Epperson left after half an hour to tend to his chores. Buzzy's air was low, so he got out to take a break and change tanks.

By noon, Buzzy had covered every square inch of the lake. As I expected, the bodies were not there.

Epperson pulled up as we were getting ready to leave and produced a picnic basket filled with ham sandwiches, chips, apple pie, and cold sodas. He told us the ham was from a pig he'd butchered the week before, and the apples were from the tree next to the house.

I was starved, and so was Buzzy. We spent the next twenty-five minutes eating and learning more about farming and grandkids than I ever wanted to know. It was a small price to pay for the great lunch.

Epperson led us back up the path. We said our goodbyes at the gate and drove back to town.

I was fighting serious food coma by the time I was back in the office. I knew I shouldn't eat the second piece of apple pie, but I hadn't had homemade pie in years. Carver's pie is good, but there's nothing like the kind mom used to make. I drew the blinds, turned off the light, and leaned back in my chair to let it pass.

I was working my way back out of a death-like snooze when the phone rang. I stretched, cleared my throat, and answered.

"Nolan."

"Detective Nolan?"

"Yes."

"Oh good. This is Pauline Crable. I tried to get you earlier, but they said you were out."

"Uh-huh."

"Anyway, I've been keeping up with the news about the, uh, things that have been cut off, and I wanted to let you know about a blond woman I saw on my way to the store this morning. I've never seen her before."

"Uh-huh."

"Well, she was getting gas at the Gas-N-Go out on Greenfield Avenue when I drove past. Her hair was long and blonde."

"Anything else?"

"She was in her car driving off by the time I drove around the block to get a better look at her."

"Was anyone with her?"

"Not that I saw."

"How tall would you say she was?"

"I don't know. Shorter than average?"

"What kind of car was she driving?"

"I have no idea. I'm not good with cars."

"What color was the car."

"Some light color. Maybe gray or green. I'm

not sure."

"Were there any circular holes on the front side panel?"

"I don't remember any, but I didn't get a good look at the car."

"Did you get the license number?"

"No."

"Do you know where she went?"

"No. It looked like she was driving out of town on Route Fourteen. I'm sorry I don't have more, but I thought you'd want to know."

"Yes, ma'am. Thanks for the call."

"You're welcome, Detective."

Pauline's blonde wasn't our perp. I was at a dead end. Dead or alive, the rodless rapists were out there somewhere, and so was the blonde. Somebody must have seen or heard something that will lead me to them. I need that somebody to contact me, now.

I reviewed files and made calls on other cases for the rest of the afternoon. I knocked off at four o'clock since I didn't seem to be getting anywhere. I thought about calling Blondie but decided against it because I didn't want to seem as eager as I was.

Con Sunderson and I had planned on having a drink after work, but I wasn't up for it today. I gave him a call to reschedule and left my office. I grabbed a Snickers on the way out and drove home, even passing up my usual visit to the Nail.

The mangy, yellow furball was hiding behind a potted plant when I got home, waiting for me to open the door so it could dash in. It was fast, but I was faster. I heard a thump, followed by an angry yowl, as I slammed the door. I smiled and pumped my fist in the air at my victory.

My dumbbells had been collecting dust under the bed for over two weeks. I stripped to my skivvies and did a ten-minute workout followed by a shower.

Cooking is something I rarely do, and today was no exception. The cupboard needed restocking, but I found a can of pork and beans hiding in the back and ate it out of the can. For my main course, I had a concoction most people find disgusting: peanut butter and pickle sandwich. Call me weird, but I like the sweet and tangy combination.

The newspaper and Richard Matheson's vampire novel, *I Am Legend*, kept me occupied until *Douglas Edwards with the News* came on at 7:30. After that, I watched *The Red Skelton Show*, followed by another chapter of vampire horrors and bed.

Chapter 18

WEDNESDAY MORNING MARKED a week since we'd found Mason Anderson's baloney pony in Shady Rock Park, and I was still no closer to solving the mystery. I'd received numerous tips about suspicious blondes, none of whom proved to be our willy wacker.

The day was trying to decide whether to rain or shine as I drove to the station. By the time I parked, the decision had been made, and large raindrops started pelting the windshield as I got out. I made it inside without getting too wet and headed to the break room for coffee. It looked like mud, so I added hot water.

Lucille heard me coming and greeted me with a middle-digit salute as I passed. We exchange our usual tongue-in-cheek insults to complete our morning ritual.

I tossed my fedora as I entered my office, and it landed perfectly on the rack. I took that to mean it would be a lucky day. I checked for Mary Francis, but she wasn't out. It seemed she wasn't part of my luck.

There were four messages stuck on the message spike. Maybe one of them would solve the dismemberment debacle. Or better yet, maybe Blondie wanted to get together.

There was no message from the blonde. I was beginning to rethink the meaning of my hat toss. The first message was from Sunderson wanting to reschedule our drink. The second was from Rosemary Anderson, wanting an update on Mason. The third was from Delores Conroy, wondering if we'd found Walt. And the last was from Officer Ben Dalton of the Franklin PD. That one got my attention, and I decided to make it my first call. Dalton picked up before I heard the phone ring.

A man, sounding like his nose was clamped off with a clothespin, answered. "Ben Dalton."

"Officer Dalton, it's Vince Nolan, Rockland PD. You left a message to call."

A loud sneeze assaulted my ear. I could almost feel the spray through the phone.

"Vince, thanks for calling, and call me Ben. Please forgive me. I've been blessed with a savage cold."

"Sorry to hear that, Ben. What can I do for you?"

"Well, it's more about what I can do for you?"

"Oh, how so?"

"I understand you spoke with my aunt recently, Cynthia Palmer."

"Yes, I did. She's a feisty one."

Another sneeze, followed by horn-like nose-blowing, and then, "You can say that again. She embarrassed me more than once as a boy, talking about female and sexual matters in front of me and my friends like we weren't there."

I wanted to say it's my friends and me but didn't. I figured he was old enough by now to have gotten it, and if not, my little speech wasn't going to make a difference.

He continued. "I visited with her yesterday. I

try to get over every couple of weeks or so. I'm the only living relative she has since my mother passed, and I know she gets lonely."

"Uh-huh."

"Anyway, she said you were trying to locate Mary McDaniels and her son. She didn't remember hearing that Mary had a son until after you left. Your conversation jogged her memory, and she remembered Evelyn Smith told her Mary did have a son named David. Cynthia asked me to be sure to tell you his name."

"Thank you and thank your aunt. But I got his name from another source."

"Hold on, there's more."

"What's that?"

"I know David McDaniels."

"You do?"

"I do. He's the new assistant pastor at my church, Piney Road Baptist, here in Franklin. Moved here about a month ago and took over the position that had been vacant for the past couple of years. He mentioned living in Rockland as a boy when he introduced himself. Nice man, kinda odd, but nice, and he sure can preach. It's like he's in a different place when he gets in the pulpit. Are you a church goin' man, Vince?"

"Not since my mom forced me to go as a kid."

"Well, never mind that. God is not a prejudiced God. He'll let you through the Pearlies just the same and forgive your sins in the process."

I'd have hung up if I hadn't wanted more information about David. I couldn't wrap my mind around blind faith and some white-robed, bearded guy floating around in the clouds. It didn't make sense to me, and I chose to use my mind rather than put it on hold and accept fantasy for reality.

"Do you know how I can contact David?"

Dalton laughed and said, "You could always come to church on Sunday." And after a silent pause during which I said nothing, he continued, "Of course, I imagine you'd like to talk with him before then."

"Correct."

"Would you like me to have him call you?"

I thought about that and decided I'd rather talk to him in person.

"No, thank you. I'll drive over. Do you have his address?"

"Hold on. I'll look it up."

The phone smacked down, followed by the rattle of a drawer being opened, then the sound of pages being turned, which I assumed was him searching through a phone book.

"Here it is. Ready?"

"Shoot."

"321 Piney Road. He lives in the rectory across from the church. You can't miss it. It's a small white house with green trim and a church parking lot on each side. He's the only one there, as the pastor is married with children and lives in a larger home a block away."

"What's the best time to catch him?"

"He's there most of the time unless he's out tending to his flock. Do you want me to tell him you're coming?"

"No, thank you. I'll take my chances."

"Alright then. Let me know if I can be of further help."

"I'll do that. You've been very helpful. Thanks again."

I left a message for Sunderson that I'd get back to him about a drink, then gave Rosemary Anderson and Delores Conroy an update on the case.

Petuski walked past my door. I motioned him in, gave him the latest on David McDaniels, and told him to be ready to leave for Franklin in twenty minutes.

I lit a smoke and poured a finger of whiskey into my coffee cup. I needed a sedative if I was going to be stuck in the car with Norb for fifty miles.

Chapter 19

PETUSKI WAS UNUSUALLY quiet on the drive to Franklin. Maybe my successful hat toss did mean luck after all. I assumed his silence was because he finally got the hint that Lila Racine wasn't going to be his girl. I felt kind of sorry for *him*, but not for Lila. With her chassis and sharp wit, she could land a big fish.

Franklin was like every other whistle-stop I'd seen. The highway served as the main street. A two-pump Texaco station with a workshop greeted visitors at the edge of town. There was a dry goods store, a mom-and-pop grocery, a cop station with one cell for the occasional drunk, an old fire truck with an all-volunteer fire department, a grade school with a combined junior high and high school, and enough churches to give all sinners the chance to get right with the Lord and ascend rather than descend when the angel of death came calling.

I turned off the highway at Piney Road and followed it three blocks to the address Officer Dalton gave me. The church was a wood frame building with stained glass windows down the sides. Six concrete steps with a wheelchair ramp on one side led up to arched double doors. A glass message board to the left of the doors gave the name of the church, the times for Sunday services, and the title of the next sermon: GIVE IT UP FOR THE LORD.

321 Piney Road sat directly across the street from the church. The paint was peeling and completely missing in spots, revealing weather-grayed wood. The address numbers were crooked, and the gravel parking lots on each side of the house were rutted and dotted with standing water from the last rain. A long, unpaved driveway next to the house ended at a dilapidated garage. It was not a wealthy parish.

I parked in front of the house and got out. Petuski followed. A piece was missing from the doorbell button. I pushed the remaining piece and heard a faint buzzing sound. After thirty seconds and no response, I pushed it again. That brought the sound of footsteps followed by the door opening, revealing a short, solemn young man with dark brown hair, sunken blue eyes, and wearing a baggy white sweatshirt and blue jeans.

"David McDaniels?"

"Yes."

I held up my shield and said, "I'm Detective Nolan, and this is Detective Petuski. Rockland PD."

He didn't say anything at first, his eyes moving back and forth between Norb and me.

"Yes, officers, how may I help you?"

"We'd like to ask you a few questions."

"I'm busy at the moment. Can this wait?"

"It'll only take a couple of minutes, and we'd rather not have to drive back again. May we come in?"

"Uh, I guess, sure."

He stepped back and let us in. The place was

dark, and the condition of the interior matched the exterior. It smelled damp with an overtone of cigarette smoke. McDaniels sat in an over-stuffed chair and motioned for Petuski and me to take the couch on the other side of the coffee table. His mouth twitched as he looked at me, then Norb, and back at me with a confused look etched on his face.

When the silence became uncomfortable, he said, "What's this about, Detectives?"

I said, "Do the names Mason Anderson and Walt Peterson mean anything to you?"

He looked down, drummed his fingers on the arms of the chair, and thought for a moment.

"No. Why?"

"There's a rumor in Rockland that those men may have raped your mother twenty years ago."

He jerked his head up, sucked in a surprised breath, and said, "What?"

"It's just a rumor at this point. We're trying to find out if it's true and thought you might be able to help us."

He stood and paced in circles behind the chair, shaking his head and flexing his fingers.

I said, "Mr. McDaniels, are you alright?"

He stopped pacing and put his hands on the back of the chair.

"That might explain it."

I said, "Explain what?"

"Why my mother changed, and why we moved."

"What do you mean?"

He sat back down in the chair and said, "My mother was always a happy, fun mom. We laughed, went for hikes in the woods, played games together. And one day, she changed. I didn't know what happened, but she seemed sad and afraid. She didn't talk to me, we didn't play games, and she was always checking to make sure the doors and windows were locked. Then we moved. She didn't tell me why. We just packed up and drove out of town."

"And you know nothing about a rape? Never heard the rumor?"

"This is the first I've heard of it."

"Your dad wasn't with you in Rockland, was he?"

"No."

"How can we get ahold of him?"

"I have no idea. I barely knew my dad. He left when I was six, and mom didn't talk about him."

"Do you have a copy of your birth certificate?"

"No."

"Where were you born?"

"Doon. About two hundred miles east of here."

"Do you remember any of your mom's friends in Rockland?"

"She didn't have many friends. There were a couple of ladies from her work that used to come over some, but I don't remember their names. And there was a guy she dated for a while, really nice guy; he used to play catch with me."

"Was his name Jake Dudeker?"

"Yeah, that's him."

"Anyone else you can think of?"

"No. That's pretty much it."

I stood, handed him my card, and said,

"Thanks for your time, Reverend. Give me a call if you think of anything that may validate the rumor."

"I'll do that."

We shook hands, and he showed us to the door. I saw the reverend watching from the window as we drove off.

I was stopped on Piney Road, signaling to turn onto the highway and head back to Rockland, when a shiny, light gray Buick Roadmaster turned in front of me and proceeded in the direction of the church. An attractive blonde was behind the wheel. Petuski and I looked at one another.

I frowned, shook my head, and said, "Nah, what are the odds?"

"Stranger things have happened, boss. We should check it out."

I did a U-ey and followed the blonde, staying a block behind. When she turned into the rectory driveway, I pulled to the curb and stopped.

The woman that got out was tall, with the kind of curves that could get a man in trouble. Trouble, I wouldn't mind getting into.

She wore a tight black dress with a matching wide-brimmed hat. Sun beans bounced off her patent leather stilettos. As she walked from the car, the roll of her derrière reminded me of the rise and fall of a gentle tide, making it hard to focus on the task at hand.

She pushed the broken doorbell button, and the door opened. She handed McDaniels what looked like car keys. They talked a bit, she laughed, and walked away. McDaniels stared at her backside until she reached the street.

When she disappeared around the corner, I pulled up to the rectory. Norb and I got out. The scent of expensive perfume still hung in the air. I wondered what a broad like her was doing in such a dead-end town.

McDaniels opened the door as we approached.

"Detectives, back so soon?"

I said, "The blonde that was just here, who is she?"

"Marci Stephenson. Why?"

"What was she doing here?"

"Returning the car. The car belongs to the church. It's for my use and any parish member who needs to borrow it. Marci has been with us for many years and sometimes uses it for her business. Is she in some sort of trouble?"

"Not at the moment. Mind if we have a look at the car?"

Wrinkles came to life on his forehead as he handed me the keys and said, "Uh, sure."

The first thing I did was walk around the car to check the tires. I checked the right-front tire last, and there it was, an outside tread block with a jagged tear and a missing corner that matched the print we found.

I looked over the hood at McDaniels. He stood on the grass with his arms folded, looking concerned. I walked up to him and said, "Did Miss Stephenson borrow the car other times during the past week?"

"Yes, several times."

"Why'd she borrow it?"

"Marci sells insurance and uses it to meet with clients."

"Does she ever keep it overnight?"

"Yes, when she doesn't get back until after dark, she'll keep it at her place."

"Did she do that this past week?"

"I believe she did a couple of times. She's been very busy lately."

"Any other blondes borrow it this past week?"

"No."

"Reverend, I'm impounding the car as evidence in a crime over in Rockland. May I borrow your phone?"

"What?"

"May I borrow your phone?"

He ran his hands through his hair and said, "Yeah."

Norb and I followed him into the house. He pointed to a phone on the kitchen counter. I dialed the station, and Lucille picked up. I gave her the rectory address and told her to send the flatbed to get the car.

McDaniels was sitting in the overstuffed chair, his right leg pumping up and down. His voice cracked when he said, "You're taking our car?"

"For now. It'll be returned when we're done."

"When will that be?"

"I don't know. Where does Miss Stephenson live?"

He looked at me and squinted. "It's Mrs. Stephenson, and she lives in the big house on Maple Street. I don't know the address. It's around the next corner to the right and two blocks down. The one with a low hedge on each side of the walk leading up to the porch."

I tossed the keys to Petuski and told him to stay with the car until I got back.

"Where are you going, boss?"

"To have a chat with Mrs. Stephenson."

Chapter 20

THE AIR WAS crisp, and a mockingbird was doing its best meadowlark imitation as I turned onto Maple Street. It was an impressive street for such a small town; the houses were large, the lawns were manicured, and the cars looked new.

Two blocks down, I spotted a big Victorian with a hedge like the one the reverend described. It was painted gray blue with white trim, had a wrap-a-round porch, two chimneys, a cone-shaped tower on the right, and a pitched roof on the left. Maple trees surrounded the property. It was the most impressive house on the street. The Stephenson's had bucks.

I stopped in front and surveyed the place. A driveway ran down the left side of the property and ended at a two-car garage that matched the architecture of the house. A pink, two-door Cadillac Eldorado Sport Coupe was parked near the garage. I wondered if it belonged to Mrs. Stephenson, and if so, why was she borrowing the parish car? I planned to find out.

When I reached the steps, a suggestive voice said, "Hello there."

I looked in the direction of the sound and saw Mrs. Stephenson reclining in a chaise lounge, sipping clear liquid from a martini glass. I glanced at my watch.

She raised her glass and said, "I know, I know, it's only ten-thirty, but I love the stuff.

Relaxes me."

"Uh-huh."

"And who are you, sir?"

I held up my shield for the second time that morning and said, "Detective Nolan. Rockland PD."

She gave me a sly smile, took a sip, and said, "This is my first. I swear."

"Uh-huh."

"What can I do for you, Detective?"

She'd kicked off her stilettos. They were on the floor next to the chaise. Her legs looked as smooth as a baby's butt, and I eyed them from her toes to the hem of her dress. I could think of lots she could do for me, but I was there on business.

"That pink boat in back your ride?"

"It is. Why?"

"Why borrow the church car when you've got that?"

She laughed.

"For business. I sell insurance, and many of my out-of-town clients are poor. I don't want them to think I'm getting rich off them."

"But aren't you?"

"Not really. I work for something to do while my husband is gone. His work takes him out of town a lot."

She held up her martini glass again.

"I make enough for this stuff and an occasional box of chocolates. It's my husband who brings home the bacon."

I climbed the last two steps and sat in the chair next to Mrs. Stephenson. She pointed to the chair and said, "Please, sit."

"I did."

She smiled and took another sip.

"Care for a drink, Detective?"

"I do, but I'm working. Thanks anyway."

She smiled, bit her lower lip, and said, "Perhaps another time."

I ignored her, but carnal thoughts raced through my head.

"Ever been to Rockland?"

"I have. Cute little town."

"When were you there last?"

She squinted, and the corner of her mouth turned up as she thought.

"Maybe two months ago. I have a client in Rockland, and I was there to service her policy."

"Who's the client?"

"Mrs. Chalmers. Dorothy Chalmers."

"What's Mrs. Chalmers address?"

"I don't know off the top of my head, but if you give me a sec, I'll check my Rolodex."

She got up and sashayed into the house. The expensive perfume scent followed her as impure thoughts did the tango in my head. I was about to undress her when the door opened, and she stepped back onto the porch carrying a Rolodex and leather-bound calendar.

She pulled out a card and said, "Here it is," as she handed it to me.

I took the card, but my eyes were on her as she slid back into the chaise. She opened the calendar and flipped through a couple of pages.

"Ah, here it is. I was in Rockland on August third."

She handed me the calendar. The entry for August third read, CHALMERS-ROCKLAND-10:30 a.m. I pulled out my notepad, made a note of the entry, and copied down Mrs. Chalmers's address and phone number. I glanced through the calendar but didn't see any other entries for Rockland.

"You haven't been to Rockland since the Chalmers meeting?"

"Nope."

"Do you know of anyone who may have borrowed the church car the past two weeks?"

"Nope."

"Do you have any other clients in Rockland other than Mrs. Chalmers?"

"Nope."

I stood and kept my eyes on Mrs. Stephenson while I lit a smoke. Her suggestive smile returned as she held out a hand with red nails, tipped her head at the Old Gold pack, and said, "May I?"

I flipped up a cig and held the pack out to her. She kept her eyes on me as she slipped the cigarette between red-painted lips. I held out my dad's sliver Zippo and lit it. She took my hand and slowly glided the flame to the smoke. She inhaled deep, turned her head slightly, and blew out a gray cloud of smoke.

"Thanks."

I knew if I didn't leave, I could lose my job. I turned, walked to the steps, and stopped.

"I'd like to get a sample of your hair."

She laughed. "From where?"

"Your head."

She wrapped a strand of blond hair around her index finger and yanked it out.

"Here ya go."

I pulled an evidence bag from my pocket, and she dropped the hair in.

"One more thing. Put out that cigarette and give it to me."

A thin crease appeared between her eyebrows as she tamped it out on the glass table next to her. I retrieved another evidence bag from my pocket and collected the butt.

Her baby blues locked on me as her tongue brushed her upper lip, and she said, "Anything else you need from me?"

I gave her a thin smile, turned, and left. As I walked down the steps, she said. "You know where I am if you change your mind."

I gave her a wave without turning around and got back in my car. As I drove back to get Petuski, I thought that Mr. Stephenson would be wise to find a job that didn't require travel.

Chapter 21

I PULLED UP in front of the rectory, and Norb got in the car. We sat there making small talk while waiting for the flatbed.

Reverend McDaniels stood at the front door, leaning against the door frame, smoking. He looked upset. Who could blame him? We were taking his ride.

Thirty minutes later, the flatbed arrived and loaded the Buick. McDaniels walked over to me as the truck drove off.

"What happens now?"

"We're taking the car to Rockland for processing. When we're done, it'll be released back to you."

"How long will that take? I depend on that car for my work."

"I understand. We'll be as quick as possible, but these things can take time. I'll let you know when we're finished, and you can come get it."

"You're not bringing it back?"

As I walked back to the green Ford, I said, "Our budget doesn't allow for that."

"Gee, thanks."

I said, "Sorry about that," got behind the wheel, and drove away.

Back at the station, Petuski went to his cubicle to do whatever Petuski does when he's not with me. I took the samples I'd collected from Marci Stephenson to the lab. I was anxious to see if she was our mutilator.

Collins was bent over his microscope, as usual, oblivious to the drab surroundings. He was focused and didn't hear me enter. I cleared my throat, and his head shot up, knocking his glasses to the tip of his nose.

"Vince, you startled me."

"Sorry about that, Timmy. I've got some things I want you to check out."

"Sure. What've you got?"

I handed him the two evidence bags, and he held them up to the light.

"Ah, this has to do with the penis case."

"You got it. I want to know if the lipstick on this cigarette is the same as on the butt and matchstick we found last week. And check the hair for a match. I'll wait."

Collins pulled two bags out of his filing cabinet and held them up to the light next to the bag with Stephenson's cigarette.

"Looks like a match but let me get them out of the bags and have a look-see with a magnifying glass."

He placed both butts and the matchstick on a glass plate, turned on his desk lamp, and pulled a magnifying glass out of his coat pocket. He kept saying uh-huh while moving the glass back and forth over the evidence.

I finally said, "Well?"

He looked at me and said, "Appears to be the same lipstick on all three. Color looks identical. But it's a pretty popular color these days. Lots of women wearing it."

I wondered how a guy that looks like Alfred

E. Neuman would know that.

"What about the hair?"

Collins labeled the bag with the Stephenson cigarette and put it in the filing cabinet with the others. He opened another drawer and brought out the bags with the hair Doc found and the hair from the motel. He continued the same quirky uh-huh routine as he studied the hairs under the microscope.

"Nope."

"Nope, what?"

"Not a match. The pigment distribution and scale patterns are different."

So Marci Stephenson wasn't the perp after all. I'd believed she was given her red lips and nails, blond hair, and the fact she was driving the Buick. It was back to the proverbial drawing board.

I told Collins we impounded a vehicle matching eyewitness accounts with tread wear identical to the print taken where the second skin flute was found. He said he'd check it out and get back to me with his findings. I thanked him and headed to my office.

The rumble in my stomach reminded me it was one o'clock, and I hadn't eaten lunch. I stopped by the break room to grab a Snickers and a pack of Planters Peanuts.

I gave my hat a toss as I walked in my office, hoping it would land on the rack as a sign of more good luck. It bounced off the wall and landed on the floor. I picked it up and put it on the hook. Superstition wasn't my thing anyway.

I lit a smoke, poured a shot of Beam into my

coffee cup, and leaned against the window frame, watching the activity on Main Street and mulling over what we had so far on the tube steak tragedy. I was pretty sure we had the perp's vehicle. We were making progress. That was a good thing. The blond slicer was out there somewhere, and we would get her sooner or later. Hopefully sooner, before she struck again.

Mary Francis hadn't made an appearance, so I finished the whiskey, lit another smoke, and called Dorothy Chalmers. I didn't believe she had anything to implicate Mrs. Stephenson, and I was right. According to her, Marci Stephenson had been sent by God himself; she'd found an auto policy with much better coverage at a significantly lower rate. Will wonders never cease?

I was reviewing the evidence we had so far when the phone rang.

"Nolan."

"Detective Nolan?"

"Speaking."

"Detective, this is John Emerson. I live over in Franklin, next door to the Baptist church."

"Hu-huh."

"Well, I saw you over at the rectory this morning, and I saw you haul off that car."

"Hu-huh."

"I read the *Rockland Gazette* and have been following what's going on over there with the missing men and the, uh, things you found. And I know you're looking for a blond woman."

That got my attention. I grabbed my notepad and a pen.

"Go on."

"Well, one night last week, I believe it was Wednesday; I was out on my porch having my nightly cigar. My wife doesn't allow me to smoke in the house. Says it gives her a headache. Anyway, I saw that Buick drive by and pull into the rectory driveway. A blond woman got out and walked into the rectory. I didn't pay it any mind at the time."

"Did you recognize her?"

"No. I never seen her before."

There was that grammar thing again, but I held my tongue.

"Do you know Marci Stephenson?"

"Oh, sure. She's a great lady. Sold me my homeowner's coverage."

"And you're sure the person you saw wasn't her?"

"Positive. This woman was about Marci's height but didn't have her figure. If you know what I mean. And her hair was longer, pulled back in a ponytail."

"What time was that?"

"Musta been around nine. That's when I'm usually on the porch."

"Did you see her leave?"

"No. I went back inside shortly after I saw her."

"Did you see Reverend McDaniels?"

"No."

"Anything else you remember about her?"

"No, it was dark, and I only saw her for a couple of seconds under the porch light when she opened the door. She was wearing a dark dress that went below her knees. I remember that."

"You saw her open the door?"

"I think so. But like I said, it was dark. It looked like it from where I was."

I took down Emerson's information, thanked him, and ended the call. My index finger tapped a staccato rhythm on the desk as I contemplated what I'd just heard. What the hell was going on? Was the good Reverend trying to protect someone? If so, why? Who?

Collins knocked on my door and entered without an invite. He was excited.

"Vince, you got the car used in the Anderson abduction for sure. I pulled his thumb print from the front passenger door handle and found a spot of blood on the front passenger seat that matches his blood type."

"Good work, Collins."

"There's more. I found a hair on the floor behind the driver's seat, and guess what?"

"It matches the other hairs."

"Yes. A perfect match."

McDaniels told me Marci Stephenson was the only blonde who had borrowed the Buick the past week. Is it possible he didn't know about the blonde Emerson saw? Or is he protecting one of his flock?

I needed to pay Reverend McDaniels another visit and check out the rectory. I was sure we had enough for a search warrant, so I gave Judge Timmerman a call and explained what we had. He agreed and said the warrant would be ready to pick up in fifteen minutes.

I buzzed Lila Racine, asked her to pick up the

warrant, and told her to grab her partner and be ready to head to Franklin as soon as she had it.

Petuski grumbled about having to go back to Franklin but gave it up when I told him about Emerson's call.

Collins was still sitting in my office grinning like he'd taken first place in a pie-eating contest. I looked at him and said, "Thanks, Timmy. You can go."

He gave me a three-finger Boy Scout salute and dashed out of the office, shouting "Yee-haw." I predict Collins will never marry.

Chapter 22

LILA STUCK HER head in my office, held up a sheet of paper, and said, "Got the warrant. We're ready to roll." She turned and left.

I grabbed my hat and coat off the rack and left the office. Petuski was in his cubicle and got up when he saw me.

I pulled out of the lot with Lila, and her partner, Larry Harris, right behind us. We drove to Greenfield Avenue and turned right toward Franklin.

Petuski kept looking over his shoulder as we sped down the highway, and I realized he was checking on Lila.

"Don't worry, loverboy, she'll be there."

He didn't say anything but whipped his head around and stared out the windshield the rest of the trip. For a detective, he doesn't have much spine.

The sun was deep in the west when I pulled up in front of the rectory. Lila parked behind me, and the four of us got out. The curtains were closed, and I couldn't tell if McDaniels was home.

We walked to the door, and I pressed what remained of the doorbell button. Getting no response, I pressed it again. The house was silent. I pounded on the door and said, "Police. Open up, Reverend."

That brought the sound of hurried steps

heading to the door. The door opened. McDaniels looked surprised.

"Detectives! Back again? What's this about?"

I held up the warrant.

"We have a warrant to search the place."

"What? Why?"

I pushed past him, and the others followed.

"You can't barge in here like that. I have rights."

"And I have a warrant. Please, sit down, Reverend."

He sat in the overstuffed chair whose springs had long ago given up supporting butts. I stood in front of him and gave him the evil eye.

"You told me no blonde other than Marci Stephenson had borrowed the Buick this past week. Why'd you lie?"

The color drained from his face. His eyes looked like cue balls.

"I didn't. I swear. She's the only one."

"Word on the street says she's not."

"That's not true. Marci's the only person who borrowed it last week."

"You sit tight. We're gonna have a look around."

He opened his mouth to protest, thought better about it, closed his trap, and slunk back in the chair like a scolded puppy.

"Lila, you and Larry take the basement. Petuski, check the kitchen. I'll take the bedroom."

Halfway down the stairs, Lila turned and said, "Boss, what exactly are we looking for?"

"Anything that smells of the blond broad being here."

"Roger that."

I slipped on my rubber gloves and opened the bedroom door. Unlike the condition of the house, it was immaculate. The twin bed had a floral-patterned spread made military-style without a wrinkle. I thought about bouncing a quarter on it.

I could hear Petuski opening and closing cupboards and moving things around. The muffled sound of voices rose from the basement. I moved to the dresser and started going through the drawers. The top one was filled with socks, underwear, and two pairs of gloves; the second with T-shirts, bed linen, and a winter scarf; the third with photo albums and old books; the bottom one was empty.

A framed photograph of a dark-haired young woman sat on top of the dresser, perhaps a girlfriend or past lover. Next to it was a wooden box. I opened the box. There was a man's gold pocket watch, two sets of cufflinks—one plain silver, the other gold with an inlaid black onyx face—and a money clip. All manly stuff.

I looked under the bed. There was nothing there except a pair of worn slippers.

The sound of a refrigerator door closing told me Petuski was still at it in the kitchen. Lila's filtered laughter rose from below, probably from one of Harris's off-color jokes.

I opened the closet door. It didn't look anything like my closet. Shirts hung to the left, short sleeves first, then long sleeves, arranged by color. Dress pants were next, again arranged by color from lights to darks. Two pairs of jeans, a jacket, a winter coat, and a black suit rounded out the wardrobe. A pair of black dress shoes, white sneakers, and black rubber boots with buckles up the front were neatly arranged on the floor. There was an umbrella leaning against one corner. Nothing that indicated a woman's presence.

I reached up to pull the light cord when I noticed a door to the attic. It was slightly ajar. There was a wooden chair against the wall by the window. I moved it to the closet and stood on it. It creaked under my weight but held. The attic door was stuck, but one good hit loosened it. Dead, dusty air rushed through the opening. The attic was pitch black.

I pulled my dad's silver Zippo out of my pocket, gave it a flick, and held it above my head. It didn't throw much light, but enough to see what was close. There was a cardboard box marked CHRISTMAS LIGHTS, a rocking chair with a busted arm, a tiffany lamp with a gaudy shade, and a large circular box that looked like a hat box.

I grabbed the round box and stepped off the chair. The box was covered with dust, and motes filled the air.

The first thing I noticed when I set the box down was several of what appeared to be fresh finger smudges on the top. They weren't mine. I only touched the sides.

I carefully lifted the lid and set it on the floor. Whatever was in the box was covered with tissue paper. I removed the paper, and there it was, a blond wig with hair the color of the hair recovered from the crime scenes. Bingo!

A bra, black dress, pointy-toed high-heels, and a makeup bag were under the wig. I unzipped the bag. There was a tube of mascara, a compact with some light tan powder in it, an eyeliner pencil, a tube of red lipstick, a bottle of red nail polish, and bobby pins. I knew what that stuff was from living with my ex, Karen.

I put the lid back on the box and walked to the living room. McDaniel's wasn't there. I went to the kitchen to see if he was with Petuski. He wasn't. I set the box on the table and told Norb what was in it.

I ran back to the living room and shouted, "He's run! Get up here!"

The sound of boots thundered up the stairs.

"Lila, you and Harris check the church, then head north. He can't be far. Norb and I will go south."

Lila and Harris were entering the church as I flipped a U-ey and slowly drove back toward the highway. It was dusk, but there was still enough light to see.

John Emmerson was standing in the street in front of his house frantically waving. I stopped, and Petuski rolled down his window.

"I saw him run out of the house. He flew by here going a hundred miles an hour. I lost sight of him about a block down."

I hit the gas and left Emmerson in midsentence. I slowed when we reached the next block and lowered my window. I could hear a dog barking farther down the street. It sounded upset.

I pulled over and stopped when we reached

the house where the dog was barking. We got out and walked to the front of the house. The dog was in the backyard.

An old woman came out on the porch as we approached. Her gray hair was rolled tight against her head with tiny pink rollers. She wore a blue terrycloth robe and fluffy blue slippers. She looked upset.

"Are you the police?"

I held up my badge and said, "Yes, ma'am."

"A man ran down my side yard a few minutes ago. I was sittin' at the table having my dinner, and he came running by. I think he's in my shed. Misty's been going off something terrible ever since."

I said, "Thank you. Go back inside. We'll take care of this."

She turned and went back in.

I told Petuski to take the left side of the house. I went down the driveway. We met in the back.

A wooden utility shed sat against the back of the property. There were no windows, and it needed paint. A German Shepard guarded the door, barking nonstop, and lunging at the door with each bark. It meant business.

Petuski and I moved to the shed with our revolvers drawn. Norb stood to the left of the door. He looked nervous. Sweat beaded on his upper lip. We turned on our flashlights.

I looked at Norb, and holding up three fingers, mouthed, "On three."

He nodded.

Without making a sound, I said, "One ... Two

... Three."

I yanked the door open and pointed my gun. The fading light wasn't enough to see inside the shed. I shined my light in and peeked around the edge of the door.

Shop tools hung on one wall, and a vise was attached to a metal bench. A shovel and rake leaned against the wall, and bags of potting soil and fertilizer were stacked near the back. I could hear whispering broken up by quiet sobs and swung my flashlight in the direction of the sound.

McDaniels was on his knees in the back corner, his hands interlaced and pressed against his chest, his head turned to the heavens, as tears streaked down his face. The whispers took full voice when my light hit him.

"Oh, God. Oh, God. Oh, my God. Please forgive me. I beseech thee. Please forgive me."

With our guns on him, I said, "Reverend."

The wailing grew louder. "I have fallen. I have fallen. Oh, God. I have sinned against thee. Oh, forgive me—"

I shouted, "Reverend."

That got his attention, and he looked at me like he just realized I was there.

I said, "Stand up, put your hands up, and slowly come out."

He continued sobbing but raised his hands and started walking out. Petuski and I backed up to give him room. Misty seemed to sense the situation was under control and stopped barking.

When he stepped out, I said, "Keep your hands up and turn around. Face the shed."

He did.

I moved toward him. Petuski kept his gun on him. I grabbed McDaniels right hand, pulled it behind him, and snapped the cuffs on him, then did the same with his other hand. The sobbing stopped when the second cuff clicked shut, and he fell silent.

Petuski holstered his gun and grabbed him by one arm. I holstered my weapon and took the other arm. I read him his rights as we moved toward the car. The old lady peeked out through the curtains as we walked past. When the light coming through the curtains hit the Reverend's face, her mouth dropped open, and a hand covered it.

Petuski secured McDaniels in the back seat while I radioed Racine and Harris with the news. They agreed to meet us at the rectory.

I moved to the back door and looked at McDaniels. He stared straight ahead, silent, with tears slowly working their way down his cheeks.

I said, "Where are they?"

No response. Tears and the rhythmic rise and fall of his chest were the only indications he was alive.

"McDaniels. Where are they?"

Nothing.

I tapped his shoulder. "Answer me." He didn't respond.

I unholstered my revolver and cocked it. Petuski's jaw dropped, and his eyes looked like cue balls. I placed the barrel of my gun against the reverend's temple. Norb sucked in a breath.

McDaniels let out a whimper and whispered,

"The house."

"What?"

"The house."

"What house?"

"The rectory. The garage in back."

I slammed the door and got behind the wheel. When Petuski was in, I turned around and headed back to the house. Racine and Harris were already there.

As I was getting out of the car, McDaniels said, "Detective."

I turned and looked at him.

He was shaking, his mouth was open, and his bottom lip quivered. "Tell them I'm sorry."

I shut the door, and the four of us hightailed it to the garage, leaving McDaniels secured in the back seat.

The garage door and the man door were both padlocked. I pulled out my revolver and fired at the lock. It blew apart.

The unmistakable stench of human excrement invaded my nose when I opened the door. The garage was dark. I ran my hand along the wall next to the door, found a light switch, and flicked it on. A single bulb came to life.

Peterson and Anderson were duct tapped to metal folding chairs in the center of the garage, their mouths gagged with pillowcases. Their pants were stained muddy red at the crotch, and their faces were etched with terror. A five-gallon bucket to the left of the chairs was the source of the stench. Candy wrappers and a crushed cereal box littered the floor.

Both men cried as we cut the duct tape and

removed the gags. They were weak from fright, lack of sleep, and little to eat for the past week. Racine and Harris each took one of Peterson's arms and helped him up. Norb and I got Anderson.

The men were too dehydrated and weak to speak as we helped them down the driveway. As we passed the car, there was just enough light to see McDaniels face pressed against the glass. He mouthed, "I'm sorry," as we walked past. Peterson mustered enough energy and saliva to hurl a loogie at the window.

Once we got the men in the back seat of Racine's car, I went into the house and got two glasses of water. They drank them down without stopping to breathe.

I told Racine and Harris to take the men to Rockland General Hospital. As they drove off, I realized that Peterson and Anderson would never play hide the sausage again. Perhaps that's what they deserved.

Petuski and I secured the house and garage and posted CRIME SCENE-DO NOT ENTER signs at the doors.

McDaniels was quiet most of the way back to Rockland. Then, almost like he was talking to himself, he spoke in a low, dead voice.

"I saw those men. I was eight years old, and I saw those men. I saw them beat and rape my mom. They didn't know I saw, but I did. They're why my mom changed, why we moved from Rockland. My mom was always fun, laughed a lot. We did stuff together. Then she got sad, and we stopped having fun. I had to leave my friends and move to a place where I didn't know any-one. My mom died because of those men. She started drinking. That's why she had the acci-dent and died. I know I said I'm sorry for what I did to those men, but I'm not. They're evil. I'm glad I did it. I did it for my mom."

We fingerprinted McDaniels and booked him into County Jail. Petuski went home, and I went to my office. The station was quiet. It was just the night duty officer, a new guy who relieved Lucille in the control room, and me. All the oth-ers were out on patrol.

I turned on the light in my office and hung up my hat and coat. I liked the quiet of the night, especially after a day like today.

The lights were off in the flower shop across the street, and Mary Francis was gone, probably home making dinner for lucky Mr. Dean.

Paul Carver was wiping down a table near the front of the cafe, and a young couple sat by the window, holding hands.

I hadn't had a drink or smoke in a while, thanks to all the excitement. I got my friend out of the bottom drawer, poured a stiff one, lit an Old Gold, and leaned back in my chair. I thought about calling Christine, but it was late, and I was tired. Thinking about her brought a smile to my face. I'll call her tomorrow.

Free Copy Of The Visitor

Visit www.stephenrossauthor.com for a FREE copy of my suspense/thriller short story "THE VISITOR" and notice of New Books/Sales

~THE VISITOR SYNOPSIS~

The morning broke like every other in the small Midwestern town of Porterville: quiet and peaceful. It's a farming community where church basement potlucks and Sunday drives in the country are the main sources of entertainment. Nothing much ever happened there until the arrival of the visitor.

Eighty-six-year-old resident Ima Plummer could not have imagined how her day would end when she awoke that fateful Wednesday.

You won't want to stop reading.

About The Author

STEPHEN ROSS practiced law until retiring in 2017. His novella, MEMOIR FROM HELL, received the 2019 Reader Views Reviewers Choice Award, and the 2019 IAN Book of the Year Finalist Award. It was praised by Reader Views as "realistic and genuine … the ending is dramatic and haunting," and by author Anthony Avina as "an emotionally charged novel that needs to be read." Stephen's other work includes, POWER LUST, a legal and political thriller set in California, a CIA thriller involving Navy SEALs, and a supernatural thriller, THE VISITOR. Born in Iowa and raised in Nebraska, Stephen now lives in San Diego, California. When he's not writing, he enjoys reading, hiking, camping, and film. He can be reached via his website at stephenrossauthor.com, on Facebook at facebook.com/stephenrosswriter, on LinkedIn at linkedin.com/in/stephen-ross-639114105, and on Twitter at twitter.com/stephenross48.

Also By Stephen Ross

Made in the USA
Middletown, DE
15 June 2021

42348760R00099